Joss turned to the silent woman sitting opposite.

Leila was the epitome of Middle Eastern modesty melded with elegant Western sophistication. From her sleek, dark chignon to the high heels that had restricted her walk to a delicate, swaying glide, she was the real thing.

Class. She had it in spades.

He didn't need the opulent black pearl pendant or the matching bracelet of massive pearls to tell him she was accustomed to luxury. She wore them with a casual nonchalance only those born to an easy life of privilege could achieve.

She seemed suitable. Her ownership of those enormously rich oil fields made her eminently suitable. It was the only reason he considered marriage: to get his hands on what would be the key to his next major venture. Besides that she had connections and the right background to be useful. Yet Joss never left anything to chance.

"I'd like to know your daughter better," he said. "Alone."

Dear Reader,

We have exciting news! As I'm sure you've noticed, the Harlequin Presents books you know and love have a brand-new look, starting this month. They look *sensational!* Don't you agree?

But don't worry—nothing else about the Presents books has changed. You'll still find eight unforgettable love stories every month, with alpha heroes, empowered heroines and stunning international destinations all topped with passion and a sensual attraction that burns as brightly as ever.

Don't miss any of this month's exciting reads:

I hope you're as pleased with our new look as we are. Drop by www.Harlequin.com to let us know what you think.

Joanne Grant

Senior Editor

Harlequin Presents

Annie West

IMPRISONED BY A VOW

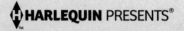

HARLEQUIN PRESENTS®

Recycling programs
for this product may
not exist in your area.

ISBN-13: 978-0-373-13171-6

IMPRISONED BY A VOW

This edition published by arrangement with Harlequin Books S.A.

For questions and comments about the quality of this book, please contact us at CustomerService@Harlequin.com.

® and TM are trademarks of Harlequin Enterprises Limited or its corporate affiliates. Trademarks indicated with ® are registered in the United States Patent and Trademark Office, the Canadian Trade Marks Office and in other countries.

Printed in U.S.A.

⊕ HARLEQUIN®
™ www.Harlequin.com

ANNIE WEST spent her childhood with her nose between the covers of a book—a habit she retains. After years spent preparing government reports and official correspondence, she decided to write something she *really* enjoys. And there's nothing she loves more than a great romance. Despite her office-bound past, she has managed a few interesting moments—including a marriage offer with the promise of a herd of camels to sweeten the contract. She is happily married to her ever-patient husband (who has never owned a dromedary). They live with their two children amongst the tall eucalypts at beautiful Lake Macquarie, on Australia's east coast. You can contact Annie through her website, www.annie-west.com, or write to her at P.O. Box 1041, Warners Bay, NSW 2282, Australia.

Other titles by Annie West available in ebook:

CAPTIVE IN THE SPOTLIGHT
UNDONE BY HIS TOUCH
GIRL IN THE BEDOUIN TENT
THE SAVAKIS MERGER

For a very special lady:

Helen Bianchin

for all your support and generosity—thank you!

CHAPTER ONE

'MARRY A STRANGER!'

'Don't sound so surprised, girl. You can't expect me to support you for ever.'

Leila bit back a retort that her stepfather's pockets were lined with the fortune he'd acquired by marrying her mother. She'd had years to learn open defiance wasn't worth the savage retribution that followed. Now wasn't the time to let him know he hadn't broken her spirit despite his best efforts.

'As for marrying a stranger, you'll wed the man I choose and there's an end to it.'

'Of course, Stepfather. I understand.' She'd heard servants' gossip that Gamil had his eye on another bride. He wouldn't want an inconvenient stepdaughter, a reminder of his previous wife, on hand. 'It's generous of you to organise this when you have so many business matters to deal with.'

Gamil's eyebrows lowered. His eyes narrowed as if he detected the sarcasm she hid behind a calm façade.

Leila had become adept at concealing emotion: grief, fear, boredom, anger…particularly anger. It burned inside her now but she held it in check. Now was not the time.

But soon! It struck her that an arranged marriage to a foreigner who'd take her far away was the chance she'd prayed for. Her previous attempts to escape had met with humiliating defeat and ever-tighter restrictions. But what could Gamil do once she was married?

It was her chance for freedom.

A thrill of excitement raced down her spine and she had to work to keep her face expressionless. Looked at like that, marrying a man she didn't know in a cold-blooded business deal was a heaven-sent opportunity.

'It goes against the grain to let him see you like this.' Gamil waved disparagingly at her bare arms and legs, her new high heels and the delicate silk dress flown in especially from Paris.

Even without a mirror, Leila knew she looked as good as she ever would. She'd been bathed, waxed, coiffed, manicured, pedicured, scented and made up by experts.

A sacrificial virgin to Gamil's ambition, primped and polished for a stranger's approval!

Leila doused a furious surge of indignation. She'd learnt long ago life wasn't fair. And if this preposterous scheme meant escape and the chance to lead her own life…

'But it's what he'll expect. He can afford the best in everything, especially women.'

Trust Gamil to see women as commodities to be bought. He was a misogynist through and through. Worse, he was pathologically controlling, revelling in his power.

His cold eyes pinioned her and Leila's skin crawled at the hatred in them. One day she'd be free of this brute. Until then she'd do whatever it took to survive.

'You'll do nothing to disappoint him. You hear?'

'Of course not.'

'And watch your tongue! None of your clever remarks. Stay silent unless asked a direct question.'

Gamil needn't have worried. Leila didn't speak when Joss Carmody entered the formal sitting room.

Her breath snagged as her gaze climbed a big frame to his rugged face. His strong features weren't chiselled but hewn, all tanned angles and sharp edges, stark lines and deep grooves. His black hair, though brushed back, curled over-long at the collar. She had the impression of unruly wildness, combed into temporary decorum, till she met his eyes and realised this man was anything but lacking in control.

He surveyed her with the keen alertness a banker devoted to his financial reports.

Joss Carmody's eyes were indigo dark, like the desert sky just before the first stars winked awake. They held hers and she felt a curious squeezing sensation high in her chest. Her pulse sped as she stood, mesmerised.

Whatever she had expected it wasn't *this*.

A moment later he turned to discuss business with Gamil. Oil of course. What else would bring an Australian resources tycoon halfway around the world? Or make him consider marrying her?

The land she'd inherit on marriage held the region's last and largest untapped oil reserves—a unique holding Gamil used to further his own prestige.

She watched Joss Carmody sit down, cradling a cup of strong coffee, effortlessly dominating the room.

Surely even tycoons took more interest in their potential brides than this? His utter indifference rankled. Surprising how much it rankled. After years under her stepfather's brutish regime it shouldn't bother her.

Why should a stranger's indifference matter? She should be grateful he had no personal interest in her. She couldn't have gone through with this if he'd looked at her the way Gamil had once stared at her mother—with that hot, hungry possessiveness.

Joss Carmody didn't see *her*, just a parcel of arid, oil-rich land. *She'd be safe with him.*

Joss turned to the silent woman sitting opposite.

Her green-grey stare had surprised him when he arrived.

He'd sensed intelligence, curiosity and, could it be, a hint of disapproval in that gaze? The idea intrigued.

Now she lowered her eyes demurely to the cup in her hand. She was the epitome of Middle Eastern modesty melded with elegant Western sophistication. From her sleek, dark chignon to the high heels that had restricted her walk to a delicate, swaying glide, she was the real thing.

Class. She had it in spades.

He didn't need the opulent black pearl pendant or the matching bracelet of massive pearls to tell him she was accustomed to luxury. She wore them with a casual nonchalance only those born to an easy life of privilege could achieve.

For a split second something like envy stirred.

He repressed it as he did anything that resembled untoward emotion. Instead he appraised her.

She seemed suitable. Her ownership of those enormously rich oilfields made her eminently suitable. It was the only reason he considered marriage: to get his hands on what would be the key to his next major venture. Besides that she had connections and the right background to be useful. Yet Joss never left anything to chance.

'I'd like to know your daughter better,' he said as Gamil drew breath. 'Alone.'

There was a flash of something in the other man's eyes. Fear or speculation? Then Gamil nodded and departed with one last, warning look at his daughter.

Joss pondered that look. Surely the old man didn't fear he'd force himself on her? As if Joss hadn't women enough to satisfy every whim!

'You've been very quiet. You don't take an interest in the oilfields you own?'

Eyes cool and clear as a mountain stream lifted to his. 'There seemed little to add.' Her English was flawless with a subtle, barely there accent that proved curiously enticing.

'You and my stepfather were engrossed in your plans.' Her charming smile didn't reach her eyes.

'You disapprove?' Sixth sense warned that her smile concealed rather than revealed.

She shrugged and he watched, intrigued as the silk slid and moulded a pleasing, feminine figure. His chosen bride was rounded in the right places, despite the fragility of her throat and wrists.

She was a necessary part of the deal yet he hadn't expected to feel more than slight curiosity about her.

The stirring of male appreciation in his belly surprised him. He hadn't expected a beauty. He permitted himself a moment's satisfaction. At least being with her occasionally wouldn't be a hardship.

'The fields will be developed.' Her low voice had a husky edge that drew his skin taut with anticipation. 'You have the resources to do that and my stepfather maintains a very close interest in the family business.'

In other words she didn't bother her head with sordid details like where her wealth came from. Why wasn't he surprised? He'd met lots like her: privileged, pampered and eager to live off the hard work of others.

'You don't work in the industry yourself? Take a personal interest in your assets?'

A spark of something lit her eyes, darkening them to stormy green. Her nostrils flared. Then her lips curved in another of those small Madonna smiles and she leaned forward gracefully to put her cup down with a click on the alabaster table.

Joss had an impression of something rippling like an undercurrent beneath her calm expression. Something elemental that made the air between them thicken, heavy with contained energy.

She spread her manicured hands. 'My stepfather takes care of all that.' Yet there was something ever so slightly out

of kilter, perhaps the way her tinted lips thinned a fraction
too much.

Then the impression was gone, leaving Joss to wonder at
his flight of fancy. An overactive imagination wasn't his style.

He was accustomed to brokering deals with men as hard
as himself. A life in mining had made him rough around
the edges, unused to dealing with delicate females, except
on the most basic level. His groin tightened as he imagined
his cool bride-to-be losing that superior air and growing hot
and eager under his touch. Satisfaction filled him, till he remembered that wasn't what he wanted from this deal. She'd
sidetracked him.

'You expect your husband to take care of business while
you enjoy the fruits of his labour?'

She darted a glance at the door where Gamil had exited.
'Forgive me. Perhaps I jumped to the wrong conclusion. I
was under the impression you wanted me as a silent partner
while you make the business decisions.' Her eyes were bright
with apparently innocent enquiry. 'Would you welcome my
interference?'

Her fine dark brows arched in eloquent surprise. For the
first time in over a decade he felt wrong-footed.

Joss stiffened. It was an illusion, of course. Far from being
out of his depth, he was running this whole scheme, including the marriage arrangements, to suit himself.

He didn't want her amateur meddling. Bad enough that
he had to put up with her stepfather's uninformed ideas until
the deal was done.

'If you have expertise in the area I'd like to hear it.' The
words were mere form. Joss worked alone. There was room
for only one commander in his empire. 'And of course your
connections to key figures across the region will be invaluable.'

'Of course.' The flat expression in her eyes, now dulling

to grey, told him she'd already lost interest. 'But I'm afraid I have no expertise in petrochemicals.'

'And where does your expertise lie?'

Again that darting glance to the door. If it weren't for her smooth serenity he'd almost believe she was worried about saying the wrong thing.

'I doubt they overlap with yours. Mine are more on the domestic scale.' She smoothed a hand over the green silk of her dress.

'Domestic as in shopping?' This desire to delve beneath her self-satisfied composure surprised him. Why the need to understand her? To label her in a box marked 'self-absorbed heiress'?

Because she was to be his wife.

After thirty-two years he was finally acquiring a spouse, if only to further his commercial interests.

Marrying went against every inclination. His life was a cautionary tale about its inherent dangers. But the commercial imperative decided him. She was a business asset.

'How did you guess I love to shop?' she cooed, stroking the pearls at her wrist. Yet the light in her eyes and that heightened spark of energy humming between them said something else went on inside that lovely head.

'Just so long as you're not under the impression I'm looking for someone to domesticate me.' He didn't want her thinking this was personal.

Her eyes rounded and a gurgle of delicious laughter broke across his senses, tightening his skin and circling his vitals. He straightened. But already she'd clamped her lips against the sound.

Domesticating Joss Carmody!

Who in their right mind would take on that challenge? He was a big, hard man, all sharp edges and steely determination. It would take someone foolishly besotted by his brooding aura of power and that sizzle of unashamed male sexuality. Someone stupid enough to believe he could ever truly care.

He wasn't the same as Gamil, she could already see that. Yet viewing those coolly calculating eyes, that formidable self-possession and monumental ego, Leila saw enough similarities.

Joss Carmody didn't have a softer side.

'Don't look so worried,' Leila said hurriedly, appalled that surprise had provoked a genuine response from her. 'The idea hadn't crossed my mind.'

'You're sure?' His straight eyebrows scrunched down in a scowl of disbelief.

Leila supposed he saw himself as a matrimonial prize. With his looks and obscene wealth women must flock to him.

Yet surely she wasn't the only one to see him for what he was: self-contained, dangerous and definitely not ready for domestication. Impatience at his all-conquering attitude blindsided her.

'Surprisingly enough, I am.' To her amazement Leila heard the rapier-sharp provocation in her tone. His expression told her he heard it too.

After years guarding every word, how could she trip herself up now? Where was her hard-won composure? Even Gamil at his worst couldn't provoke an outburst these days. It was vital she play to the Australian's expectations if the marriage was to go ahead.

'So what did you envisage, Leila?' His voice dropped half an octave, slowing on her name. He rolled it around his mouth, almost as if savouring it.

Fine hairs rose on her arms and nape. No man had ever said her name like that. A challenge and an invitation at the same time.

Heat flushed her throat as she realised she'd stepped into perilous waters. He didn't threaten like Gamil, but she sensed danger in his sultry invitation. Not the danger of physical punishment but of something more insidious.

Her lack of experience with men told against her now.

She blinked. Gamil was no doubt hidden beyond the doorway, sifting each word, ready to mete out punishment for errors.

The laugh had been a mistake. She'd read it in Joss's surprise. Yet she couldn't regret it. He deserved to be shocked from his insufferable self-satisfaction, even if her stepfather made her pay later.

'I thought you were interested in my inheritance, not me personally.' She kept her tone even, holding his gaze, refusing to reveal how much hinged on his response.

After a moment he nodded brusquely. 'I'm not after an heir and I have no interest in playing happy families.'

At least he didn't expect intimacy. Relief swelled.

She'd wondered whether, when it came down to it, she would be able to sell herself into an intimate relationship in order to escape. Had wondered too about the logistics of disappearing as soon as they were married to avoid giving herself physically to a man she didn't want. Now it seemed she wouldn't have to.

This was pure business. He'd gain the oil reserves, while Gamil gained income and status through his new son-in-law.

She was supposed to be thrilled by Joss Carmody's offer of matrimony. Though come to think of it there'd been no offer. It had been a deal done between power-hungry men.

She squashed instinctive outrage as a luxury she couldn't afford.

'I don't want a wife who will cling or make demands.'

'Of course not.' She couldn't imagine him accepting emotional ties. Nor did she want any.

'So tell me, Leila—' he leaned closer, his voice a deep thread of sound that shivered across her flesh '—why do you want to marry *me*?'

Her brain froze as she watched those firmly sculpted lips shaping her name, feeling again that tremulous shock of disturbance deep inside.

Then she breathed deeply, her mind clicking into gear, considering and discarding possibilities.

Tell him what he expects to hear and seal the deal.

'For what you can give me.' His almost-imperceptible nod confirmed she was on the right track, feeding him the response he expected. 'To see the world and live the life of a billionaire's wife. Bakhara is my homeland but it's rather… confining.' Wry laughter threatened at the understatement and she bit her cheek, using pain to counter weakness. It was a trick Gamil, if only he'd known it, had inadvertently taught her over the years, with his regime of punishments for imagined infringements. 'Married to you my life will change for ever.'

Dark eyes surveyed her so closely she saw the exact moment he made up his mind. His lips pursed and his eyes gleamed approvingly.

Joss Carmody knew what he wanted. A wife who wouldn't clutter his life. A woman who'd marry him for his wealth and prestige. A woman who would shop and amuse herself while he got on with what interested him: making even more billions of dollars. Money drove him. Nothing else.

What would he do if he realised he meant just one thing to her?

Escape.

'He's late!' Gamil paced the courtyard, his heavy tread careless of the exquisite mosaics Leila's ancestors had installed and the carefully nurtured grass by the long mirror pool, a lush green bed in a land of scarce rainfall and high temperatures.

'What did you say to him?' He spun round, spittle spraying Leila's cheek. 'It must have been you. Everything else was settled. There's no reason for him to cry off unless you put doubt in his mind.'

His angry countenance filled her vision but she stood steadfast, knowing better than to retreat before his fury.

'You heard all that passed between us,' she said levelly. Too much in fact. Her temerity in laughing at Joss Carmody's self-conceit had earned her weeks of punishment on bread and water. Fortunately her rations had been increased this week so she wouldn't be too weak to say her vows.

'That I did.' Ire mottled Gamil's complexion. He leaned forward, his stale breath hot on her face. 'I heard you play word games! Obviously that was enough to make him have second thoughts. And now...' Gamil gritted his teeth and turned away.

'How will I hold my head up if you're jilted by such a man? Think what it will do for my reputation, my prospects at court! I have plans...'

He stalked to the other end of the courtyard, muttering. His hands clenched and unclenched as if ready to throttle someone.

Her stepfather rarely resorted to physical violence, preferring more subtle methods. But she had no illusions she was safe if he felt himself goaded too far.

Leila pressed clammy hands together. If only Joss Carmody would thrust open the ornamental doors and stride into the courtyard.

Never had an unwanted bridegroom been so eagerly awaited.

Fear churned her stomach. Was Gamil right? Had the Australian cried off? What, then, of her plans for independence and the career she'd always wanted?

No! She couldn't think like that. There was still time, though he was ninety minutes late and the whispering guests had already been ushered into the salon for refreshments.

Heat filled the courtyard. Leila stiffened her weary spine against the frightening compulsion to admit defeat.

How many more years could she take? This last bout of solitary confinement had almost broken her.

Gamil had broken her mother, destroying her vibrant optimism and love of life. Leila had watched her change from an outgoing, charming beauty, interested in everyone and everything. In a few short years she'd transformed from a society hostess par excellence and an asset to her first husband's brilliant diplomatic career to a faded, downtrodden wraith, jumping at shadows. She'd lost the will to live long before illness had claimed her.

Leila tipped her head up, feeling the sun on her face. Who knew how long before she'd feel it again?

Despite the gossamer-fine silks, the lavish henna decorations on her hands and feet, the weight of traditional gold jewellery at her throat and ears, Leila was no pampered princess but a prisoner held against her will.

If Joss didn't show, standing here in the open air might be the closest she'd come to freedom till she came of age at twenty-five in another sixteen months.

'What are you doing outside in the heat?' The dark voice sidled through her thoughts and shock punched deep in her solar plexus.

He was here!

Her eyes snapped open. At the sight of his imposing frame, his don't-mess-with-me jaw and piercing eyes, Leila found herself smiling with relief. Her first genuine smile in years. It stretched stiff facial muscles till they hurt, the sensation strange in her world of guarded emotion.

Joss halted, struck anew by her curious combination of fragility and composure. That hint of steel in her delicate form. She looked thinner, her neat jaw more pronounced and her wrist narrow as she raised a hand and the weight of gold bangles jingled.

Her eyes opened, the pupils wide in clear grey depths. Then as he watched velvety shades of green appeared, turning her gaze bewitching.

She smiled. Not that tiny knowing smile of last month, but a broad grin that made something roll over in the pit of his stomach.

Ensnared, he drank in the sight of her, the warmth in her frank appraisal, the pleasure that drew him closer.

Heavy scent filled his nostrils, a dusky rose that clogged his senses. It wasn't right on her. But then this woman, decked in the traditional wedding finery of her land, seemed so different from the one whose verbal sparring had intrigued him weeks ago.

'I was waiting for you.' There was no rancour in her voice but her eyes held his as if awaiting his explanation.

A hot spurt of sensation warmed his skin. Guilt?

Gamil hadn't dared voice reproach when Joss arrived, knowing as countless others had before him that Joss lived by his own rules, at his own convenience. He didn't give a damn if his priorities didn't match anyone else's.

Business came first with him—always. The urgent calls he'd taken this morning had required immediate action whereas a wedding could be delayed.

Yet seeing her expression, Joss had the rare, uncomfortable feeling he'd disappointed. It evoked memories of childhood when nothing he did had lived up to expectations. His tough-as-nails father had wanted a clone of himself: utterly ruthless. His mother…just thinking of his mother made him break into a cold sweat. He shoved aside the dark memories.

'You waited out here? Couldn't you have waited in the cool? You look—' he bent closer, cataloguing her pallor and the damp sheen on her forehead and upper lip '—unwell.'

Her smile slid away and her gaze dropped. Instantly the heat in his belly eased.

'My stepfather made arrangements for the ceremony to take place here.' She gestured across to a fanciful silk canopy. Joss dragged his gaze from her. There were pots of heavy-scented roses, ornate gilded furniture, garlands of flowers, rich hand-woven rugs and gauzy hangings of spangled fabric.

'Clearly he's not familiar with the idea that less is more,' Joss murmured.

A choked laugh drew his attention, but Leila was already turning away in answer to a brusque command from her stepfather. Beneath the flowing silk of her robe, she was rigid. She paced slowly, as if reluctant.

Joss watched the interchange between them. One so decisive and bossy, the other unnaturally still. His hackles rose.

He stalked across the courtyard to join his affianced bride. For reasons he couldn't fathom, his pleasure at today's business coup faded. He felt out of sorts.

The wedding was almost over. The ceremony had been short, the gifts lavish and the feast massive, though Leila hadn't been able to indulge much. After short rations for so long, she felt queasy even smelling rich food and the room had spun if she'd moved too quickly.

She'd had to work to repress excitement. Soon she'd be out of her stepfather's house for good.

She'd be the wife of a man who wouldn't impose himself on her. He'd take her away from here, his only interest in the oilfields she'd inherited. They'd negotiate a suitable arrangement—separate residences and then eventually a discreet divorce. He'd keep the land and she'd be free to—

'Leila.' His deep voice curled around her and she turned to find him watching, his dark gaze intent. He held out a heavy goblet.

Obediently she sipped, repressing a cough at the heady traditional brew. A concoction designed, it was said, to heighten physical awareness and increase sexual potency.

Joss lifted the cup, drinking deeply, and the crowd roared its approval. When he looked at her again his gaze as it trawled her was different. Heat fired under her skin. It felt as if he caressed her: across her cheek, down her throat then lingering on her lips.

Something flared in his eyes. Speculation.

Sharply she sat back, fingers splayed on the chair's gilt arms as she braced herself against welling anxiety.

'You make a beautiful bride, Leila.' The words were trite but the warmth in his eyes was real.

'Thank you. You're a very attractive groom.' She'd never seen a man fill a suit with such panache or with that underlying hint of predatory power.

Joss's mouth stretched in a smile. A moment later a rumble of laughter filled the space between them. 'Such praise! Thank you, wife.'

She didn't know if it was the unexpected sound of his amusement or the velvet caress of his gaze but Leila felt an abrupt tumble of emotions.

Suddenly this marriage didn't seem so simple. She'd spent so long fretting about escape, focused on getting through the marriage ceremony. Now it hit her that perhaps he had other ideas on what happened after the wedding.

Leila shivered.

For the first time she realised Joss Carmody might be dangerous in ways she'd never considered.

CHAPTER TWO

'THERE'S BEEN A CHANGE of plan,' Joss said as the limousine surged forward. 'We're going straight to the airport. I need to be in London.'

He turned to his bride, surprised to find her attention fixed on the back of their driver's head. She didn't acknowledge the wedding guests clustered to see them off. She didn't even lift an arm to wave to her stepfather, standing at the ornate gates to the road.

With her gold-encrusted headscarf pulled forward, obscuring her profile, Joss only caught a glimpse of her straight, elegant nose.

'Leila?' He leaned forward. 'Did you hear me?'

Her hands were clasped in her lap, the knuckles white.

What now? He didn't have time for feminine games. He'd already given up a whole afternoon playing the attentive bridegroom.

'Leila, look at me.'

The command did the trick and she turned instantly. Her eyes were a smoky grey, wide and unfocused. Her lips were flattened and her skin pale.

Impatience flared. What was the problem? Something he'd have to deal with no doubt when all he wanted was to get back to business.

He should have known marriage would complicate his

plans! It had gone against every instinct to acquire a wife, though the business benefits had outweighed the negatives.

Yet with the impatience came an unfamiliar pinprick of concern. 'What is it, Leila? Are you unwell?'

'No.' The single word was husky, as if issued from a dry mouth. 'I'm never sick.' Her lips moved in a shadow of a smile.

Joss remained silent. Something was definitely amiss. He told himself that so long as it didn't affect him it didn't matter. He wasn't his wife's keeper. But curiosity stirred. More, he acknowledged a faint but real desire to ease what he guessed was pain behind those beautiful blank features.

'Would you like to stop the car?' After the interminable wedding, he couldn't believe he was offering to delay further. 'We could go back inside and—'

'No!' Her voice was strident, her face no longer blank but animated at last.

'No,' she repeated, her voice softer. 'That's not necessary. Let's just…go.'

Was it his imagination or was that a plea in her voice?

'As you wish.' He leaned forward and opened the limousine's bar fridge. Ignoring the foil-topped bottle of Cristal and gold-rimmed champagne flutes some romantically inclined staffer had placed there, Joss reached for bottled water. Unscrewing the cap, he passed it to her.

She took it but didn't make a move to drink. Was she waiting for a cut-crystal tumbler as well? He wouldn't be surprised, given the pampered life she'd led.

'Drink,' he ordered. 'Unless you'd prefer me to call a doctor?'

Instantly she raised the bottle and sipped. She paused and drank again, colour returning to her cheeks.

Now he thought about it, he couldn't remember her drinking at the reception, except when he'd raised the goblet to her lips. Nor had she done more than peck at her food.

'You need food.' He reached for the gourmet snacks beside the bar.

'No, please.' She shook her head. 'I'm not hungry. The water is fine.'

Joss's eyes narrowed on the sharp angle of her jaw revealed as she tipped her head back. Her slim throat worked as she took a long pull from the water bottle.

'I'm feeling much better now.' This time she almost convinced him. Her voice was steadier, her gaze direct. 'What were you saying about a change of plans?'

'We're not staying in Bakhara,' he responded, watching her narrowly. 'Something has come up. I need to be in London tonight.'

He could go alone. But he'd just acquired a hostess with impeccable breeding, social standing and poise who'd be a valuable asset in his new business dealings. He intended to make use of her.

Besides, he saw no point in sabotaging the polite fiction they were a couple. Leaving his bride on her wedding night would be inconvenient front-page news. If she was to be of use to him, it would be at his side.

'London? That's marvellous!'

Leila's incandescent smile hit him hard. It wasn't the polite, contained curve of the lips she'd treated him to before but a wide brilliant grin. It was like the one she'd turned on him when he'd arrived a few hours earlier.

Its impact set his pulse tumbling.

She wasn't beautiful. She was stunning.

How had he not realised? He'd thought of her as coolly elegant. Now her sheer dazzling exuberance rocked him.

With colour flushing her cheeks and throat, her lips parted in pleasure and her eyes dancing, she beguiled in a way no blatantly sexy supermodel ever could.

An unfamiliar sensation stirred in his chest and Joss was stunned to realise it was his lungs struggling to pump oxygen. Perhaps whatever ailed Leila was catching. His reaction to her was unprecedented.

'I'm glad you're so excited about a trip to London.' His voice was gruff.

Joss had never been overcome by attraction to a woman. It was the way he was made. *An emotional wasteland*, one mistress had accused in tears after he'd crushed her fanciful hopes of happily ever after.

He desired women. He enjoyed the pleasure they provided. But they never caused a ripple in his life.

As for emotions…he'd been cured of those in his youth.

Growing up in a dysfunctional family, learning early the destructive power of so-called 'love', Joss had never wanted anything like it again. No emotions. No entanglements. No dependants. His gut clenched at the very idea of kids and a clinging wife. Only a deal like this, based on sound business requirements and no emotional expectations, could convince him to marry.

Joss was a loner to the core.

'You've spent time in London, I believe?' He should know more about the woman who was to be his hostess.

She nodded, her smile barely abating. 'I was born there. Then we moved to Washington when my father took another diplomatic posting, then Paris and Cairo with short stints in between in Bakhara. We moved back to Britain again when I was twelve.'

'And you enjoyed it?' That much was obvious. 'You have friends to catch up with there?'

Her smile faded and her gaze swept from his. It struck Joss she'd had her eyes fixed firmly on him all through their conversation. He felt an odd…lack now she'd turned away.

She shrugged. 'Perhaps.'

'So it's the shopping you're looking forward to?'

'No, I…' She swung to face him, but this time her lashes veiled her eyes. Did she realise how sexy that heavy-lidded look was? No doubt it was one she'd practised. 'Well, of course, shopping is part of the London experience.' Her mouth curved in a smile but this time it didn't have the same wattage. Its impact didn't resonate inside his chest.

Good. That earlier response was an aberration. He had no intention of feeling anything for his wife other than satisfaction at the benefits she brought to his balance sheet: fuel resources to exploit and her personal connections in the region.

'I can see you'll enjoy yourself in London.' He'd wondered if he'd face an emotional plea to extend their stay in Bakhara after the wedding. It pleased him she was so reasonable. They'd deal perfectly together. 'The jet is fuelled and ready to go as soon as we reach the airport.'

'That's—' She stiffened and sucked in a gasp. 'My passport! I can't—'

'You can. Your passport is waiting at the plane.'

'Really?' She leaned forward, her eyes searching. 'You had no trouble getting it from…from the house?'

'My staff did it. I assume there was no difficulty.' Joss surveyed her curiously. He'd almost swear that was shock on her face. 'Is something wrong?'

'Wrong?' Her voice stretched high. 'Of course not. I just…' She shook her head. 'Everything's perfectly fine, thank you.' She turned away to watch the retreating city as the car sped towards the airfield. 'How long till we reach the plane?'

Joss leaned back in his seat, intrigued by the flicker of emotions he'd seen in his wife's face. He'd pegged her for a woman of unruffled sophistication, with the poise of a socialite who took world travel and privilege for granted.

It was a surprise to find there was more to Leila than he'd expected. If he had the inclination he'd almost be tempted to discover more.

Almost.

He had higher priorities than learning about his wife on anything other than a superficial level.

* * *

'We're almost there.'

His words were music to Leila's ears.

Escape, not only from her stepfather's home, but from Bakhara, seemed too good to be true. Though she loved her homeland, she wouldn't feel safe from Gamil till she was a continent away. She'd expected to stay in the country a few more weeks and had fretted over the possibility Gamil would find a way to convince Joss to leave her behind when he went.

The few times over the years when she'd succeeded in escaping the house she hadn't got far. Gamil's staff had found her and forcibly hauled her back, and each time the punishments had grown more severe. Gamil's money and legal power as her guardian gave him control over her till she married or turned twenty-five. He'd restricted her travel, education, friendships and money.

Even now she was married, she'd feared he'd find some way to stymie her escape. But now—freedom! She could taste it on her tongue, sweet and full of promise.

The thrill was almost enough to dispel the strange queasiness she felt.

It had been over twelve months since she'd been allowed out of the front door. The clenching spasm of stomach muscles, the panic that had grabbed her throat and made her heart race as she'd left the house, had hit out of nowhere. She hadn't even been able to wave farewell to the guests, every fibre concentrated on conquering that sudden tension.

As if she'd been *afraid* to step into freedom.

Ridiculous! For years she'd done nothing but plan how to get away.

It was just the rich food after sparse rations that had turned her stomach. The heavy scents clogging the air at the wedding feast and the buzz of conversation after months of monastic silence that made her dizzy.

Or maybe it was excitement at being so close to escape.

Fear that at the eleventh hour it would all go wrong. She knew firsthand how Gamil liked to toy with his victims—hold out the illusion of liberty then yank it away. She'd watched it happen to her mother too. Each time Leila had vowed not to let him best her. But she shuddered, remembering.

'Are you cold?'

'Not at all.'

Nothing could stop her boarding that plane. This was the first day of her new life away from the man who'd made her world, and her mother's, hell. Soon she'd put her plans into action. Set herself up with the money she got on marriage and see about resuming her studies. She'd build a new life without ever needing to ask anyone's permission again.

Joy flooded her. This was real. Joss had already secured her precious passport. How often had Gamil taunted her that he kept it under lock and key?

The limousine was ushered through a gate and onto the airfield. Moments later they drew up near a sleek jet. Staff waited to see them aboard.

'Ready?' The deep rumble of her husband's voice tickled Leila's spine, leaving her skin tingling. But, she reassured herself, he was husband on paper only. The instrument of her freedom.

'Ready.' Eagerly she pushed open the door before the chauffeur reached it.

Warm, desert-scented air wafted into the car as she slid from the seat. She nodded her thanks to the uniformed driver, turned to face the crew lined up at the base of the steps and grabbed the car door as her knees abruptly crumpled.

The world swooped around her: the sky vast, almost endless as it tilted and stretched towards a far distant horizon. It was so huge, so empty, as if it had the power to suck her up into its immense nothingness. Sick heat beat at her temples.

Her pulse raced as her heart catapulted against her rib cage. In her ears she heard the roar of pounding blood.

A nameless, dragging terror clawed at her. She knew it would press her down till that infinite space swamped her, expelling the last of the air from her labouring lungs.

Leila couldn't breathe. Yet she fought to stay on her feet. She saw the chauffeur say something then Joss was in front of her. His mouth moved. His brow pleated in a scowl.

He might have been behind glass. Everything was distant but for the heat, the weight of the very air pushing at her, and the tandem crashing thud of her heart and lungs as panic seized her and her stomach churned.

Adrenalin surged as she fought the impulse to fling herself back into the car. Into that small cocoon of safety that beckoned so tantalisingly.

She wouldn't do it.

She wasn't going back, no matter what!

Yet it was all she could do to keep her feet on the ground, her hands limpet-like on the door.

'Leila!' This time she heard Joss. There was concern in his brusque tone. 'What is it?'

She dragged in a deep breath and with furious effort straightened her shoulders. She lifted her chin, swallowing with difficulty, her throat as dry as the great inland desert.

Joss's dark gaze held hers, reminding her she was strong. She'd survived years with her dangerously controlling stepfather. She'd got through a farce of a wedding that was all about business, not love. Surely she could walk to the plane.

The thought of being taken back to the capital, perhaps to her old home and her stepfather's tender mercies, was a douche of ice water on overheated flesh.

'Sorry,' she said in an unfamiliar voice. 'My legs are stiff from sitting so long.' She tried to smile but it was more of a grimace. 'I'll be okay in a minute.' At least her voice was merely hoarse now, not wobbly.

For answer Joss turned and said something to his staff, who dispersed out of sight.

Leila drew another breath. Whatever this unnamed fear, it wasn't rational. It could be overcome. She took a tentative step, still holding the car door. Her legs were made of concrete, so heavy, yet shaking and weak as water.

She took a second step towards the jet. Only twenty paces to the stairs. She could manage that.

With a shuddering breath Leila forced her cramped fingers to release the door. Willing herself on, she paced towards the plane.

Out of nowhere strong arms wrapped round her, scooping her up. They hefted her against a solid body that smelled of soap and citrus and what could only be the spicy scent of male flesh. A thread of heat eddied through her, warming her frozen body.

The arms tightened and she felt the reassuring thud of Joss's heart against her: steady, calm. Reassuring.

In that moment her instinctive protest faded away.

It didn't matter that she hated the idea of needing help. Or that Joss acted simply because he couldn't leave his bride collapsing on the tarmac.

For the first time since her mother's death Leila knew the comfort of being held. The shock of it helped clear her pounding head.

'Relax,' Joss said in an even tone as if dealing with a half-fainting female didn't faze him. Perhaps he was used to women swooning at his feet! 'I'll have you somewhere quiet in a moment.'

'I can walk. I want to board the plane!' She jerked her head up and found herself with a close-up view of his solid jaw and a full lower lip, incongruous in such a harshly defined face yet somehow right. Midnight-blue eyes bored into her, alight with speculation. Straight eyebrows tilted high towards his hairline as if he registered her desperation.

Anxiety still jangled like a drug in her bloodstream but she met his scrutiny with all the dignity she could muster.

'Please, Joss.' It was the first time she'd said his name and it slipped out with an ease that surprised her. 'I'll be fine once I'm aboard.'

He hesitated and Leila's nerves stretched to breaking point. She watched his brow furrow as he scrutinised her minutely. 'Very well. The jet it is.'

Leila dragged in the breath to fill her empty lungs. 'Thank you.'

She shut her eyes and tried to regulate her ragged breathing, willing her pulse to slow. She sensed him move but didn't open her eyes. It was enough to feel those hard muscles holding her, the sense of safety seeping slowly into her taut body.

She didn't let herself question why she felt safe in the arms of a stranger.

'I'm sorry,' she whispered. 'I'm not usually given to...' What? What was wrong with her? 'Usually I can even walk and make conversation at the same time.'

A huff of laughter riffled the hair on her forehead. 'No doubt. Don't forget I've seen you play hostess, deal with an unfamiliar husband in front of hundreds of guests at a never-ending wedding and maintain your poise without batting an eyelid.'

Leila's eyes popped open at the note of wry humour in that deep suede voice. It...appealed to her.

She'd thought Joss Carmody too dour for humour. Too focused for sympathy, especially for a wife he didn't want. She'd been sure when he looked at her all he saw was a vast tract of land awaiting development.

'That was a short wedding celebration by Bakhari standards,' she murmured, concentrating on his face and not the vast sky beyond his shoulder as he ascended the stairs to the plane. 'We got off lightly.'

Gamil had been furious, wanting to display his wealth and important son-in-law to the cream of society. He'd surpassed himself in ostentatious displays of riches that would have made her parents cringe. No wonder she'd felt ill. It *must* have been the heavy food.

Leila felt a solid shoulder shrug against her as Joss stepped sideways through the door. Strange how she didn't mind in the least the alien sensation of being clasped so close to him.

'I had places to be. I couldn't stay feasting for day upon day.'

'Of course not. Very few people insist on such traditions any more.'

She took a deep breath of cool air and surveyed the luxurious private jet. Already she felt better. Maybe after years locked away she'd simply lost her ability to deal with the Bakhari heat. The explanation buoyed her.

'I can stand now. Thank you. I feel all right.'

Joss tilted a look from his superior height, scouring her face as if penetrating her secrets. His expression gave no hint of his thoughts. But then he was a self-made multibillionaire. He'd perfected the art of keeping his thoughts to himself.

A flicker of unease trembled under her skin. What did he see as he watched her? A business asset or something else?

Leila pushed her palm against his collarbone, trying to lever some distance between them. It didn't work, only making her aware of his unyielding strength. Held in his arms, she suddenly felt not so much protected as vulnerable. Puny against his formidable masculinity.

It made her uneasy.

His gaze dipped to her mouth and her lips tingled as if she'd eaten chilli.

'Joss! I said I can stand.' Suddenly it was imperative he release her. She'd felt light-headed before but this was different. Something she didn't want to explore. Something to do with *him*.

Smoothly he put her down, watching her intently.

Fortunately the strength had returned to her legs. She was

herself again, able to walk, spine straight and legs steady, to the lounge chair the stewardess indicated.

Sitting straight despite its encompassing luxury, Leila turned to the hovering stewardess.

'I'd like some water, please. And do you have anything for travel sickness?'

'Of course, madam.' The woman bustled away.

If Leila tried hard enough she might convince herself it was motion sickness she'd experienced out there after her first trip in a vehicle in ages. Or the effects of heat.

She watched Joss sit on the other side of the cabin. His gaze didn't leave her as she took the medication and a healthy slug of water.

His scrutiny made her uneasy. It wasn't like Gamil's, which had always made her flesh crawl. But Joss's steady regard seemed to strip her bare. Surely he couldn't see the tumble of elation and anxiety she strove to hide? Concealing what she felt had been a matter of survival under Gamil's cruel regime and she'd become adept.

Deliberately she put her head back and closed her eyes, reassured by the hum of the engines starting.

When finally she felt the plane take off she opened them to see Joss, head bent over a stack of papers, his pen slashing an annotation across the page.

Relief welled up inside her. He'd forgotten her, his curiosity had been temporary. Once they reached London he'd forget her entirely.

She turned to see Bakhara drop away and exhilaration filled her. Her new life had just begun.

CHAPTER THREE

'I SEE YOU'VE made yourself at home.'

Joss sauntered into the kitchen. The sight of his wife setting a kettle to boil made the huge, functional room seem domestic, almost cosy.

It was the last place he'd expected to find her. Given the number of servants in her old home he'd imagined her reclining in bed and summoning staff to wait on her.

Leila swung round, eyes wide, and he felt the impact of her clear gaze like a touch. Intriguing. Yesterday he'd put the sensation down to curiosity and a tinge of concern when she'd all but fainted at his feet.

'You surprised me,' she said in a husky voice that purred through his belly. 'I didn't expect to see you here.'

Joss shrugged. 'I've been known to make my own coffee occasionally.' Hell, he'd spent enough time batching in rough-and-ready outback accommodation to know his way around a kitchen. He could feed a whole shift of hungry miners if need be. Plain, hearty fare that stuck to the ribs, not the sort of fancy delicacies a society princess like Leila ate. She was like his mother had been—used to being waited on.

'I meant I didn't expect to see you in the apartment.' As his brows rose she added, 'Not at this time of day. It's only early afternoon.'

'And tycoons never take time off?' He watched her gaze skitter away across the gleaming floor before returning to his.

The connection ignited a tiny spark of sensation.

Joss ignored it. He was good at ignoring unimportant things. Things that didn't figure in his plans.

'I understand you're a self-made man. You can't have got where you are without working long hours.'

So, she'd been interested enough to find out that much.

'You're right.' He strolled across the room, peeled off his jacket and dropped it on a stool near the enormous island bench. 'My working hours are long.'

There was an understatement! He didn't bother explaining that he enjoyed the cut and thrust of expanding his empire. That he revelled in the challenges of business despite the highly efficient teams he employed.

Business was an end in itself, giving total satisfaction. His commercial success gave him a purpose nothing else could. There was always a new goal, inevitably harder, more satisfying than the last. Hence his move into new territories with this Bakhari deal and his recent mining acquisition in Africa.

'I'll be working tonight, video conferencing with Australia, and I leave tomorrow to deal with a crisis.' The rest of his London meetings would have to wait. An oil-rig accident took priority. 'In the meantime it's time for us to talk.'

'Good idea.' Leila nodded but her shoulders looked stiff.

Why was she tense? Because of him? Or was she ill again? He frowned.

Last night, arriving in Britain, she'd barely stirred when they landed, knocked out apparently by the medication she'd taken. He'd had to carry her to the car and again from the basement car park to the apartment.

He'd left it to his efficient housekeeper to get her to bed. Then he'd put in a couple of hours in his private gym and study before retiring in the early hours.

Yet instead of sleeping instantly as he'd trained himself to do, Joss had lain awake pondering the enigma that was his wife.

There'd been no mistaking her fragility as he'd held her in his arms. She'd weighed next to nothing when he'd scooped her up and onto his jet. He'd felt the bony jut of her hip and the outline of her ribs.

That had stirred long-buried memories. Of Joanna at fifteen—all skin and bone, turning in on herself rather than facing the selfish demands of their parents. Parents who'd never given a damn about either of their children, except as weapons in their vindictive, ongoing battle against each other.

Holding Leila, feeling the tremors running through her, evidence of the weakness she strove to hide, Joss had been hit by a surge of protectiveness he hadn't known since he was ten, wanting to save the big sister who had wasted away before his eyes.

But Leila wasn't Joanna. Leila wasn't some wounded teenager. She was a grown woman, well enough to sell herself for an easy life of wealth.

It was no concern of his if she'd overdone the pre-wedding dieting. Yet he found himself checking. 'You're better today?'

'Much better, thank you. The wedding preparations must have tired me more than I knew.'

The kettle boiled and clicked off. 'Would you like something? I'm making chamomile tea.' She favoured him with one of those small, polite smiles. The perfect hostess.

'Sounds appalling. I'll stick with coffee.' He strode to the door, ready to call his housekeeper, only to find her scurrying towards him.

'What can I get you, Mr Carmody?'

'Coffee and a sandwich. My wife will have chamomile tea and…?' He raised an interrogative brow.

'Nothing else, thanks. I'm not hungry.'

Joss surveyed the demure beige silk dress hanging loose on her. She'd lost weight since they first met. Then she'd been slim but rounded in all the right places. Now even the line of her jaw was stark, too pronounced.

His eyes narrowed. It wasn't just the weight loss that disturbed him. She looked…drab. He was no fashion expert but even he could see that shade leached the colour from her face. The dress was completely wrong, suited to an older woman rather than a young and pretty one.

At least her legs were as delectable as he recalled.

At their first meeting he'd been distracted, enjoying the counterpoint of her sexy legs and lush mouth with her composed, almost prim demeanour. Plus there'd been those tiny flashes of spirit that had reassured him she had the capacity to hold her own as the society hostess he required.

She was a fascinating combination of intellect, beauty and cool calm. Or she would be to a man who allowed himself to be fascinated.

Joss wasn't in that category. He had no intention of disrupting a sound business arrangement with anything like an intimate relationship.

He strictly separated his business and private lives. Though physical intimacy probably rated in the business side of his life: sex for mutual pleasure plus the expensive gifts and five-star luxury he provided to whatever woman he chose to warm his bed.

'Mr Carmody?'

Joss found his housekeeper surveying him curiously.

'I leave it to you, Mrs Draycott. Just bring a selection that will tempt my wife's appetite.'

Leila's stare sharpened. That look provoked a tiny sizzle of pleasure in his gut, like anticipation at the beginning of a new venture.

'Of course, sir.'

'We'll be in the small sitting room.'

Leila held his gaze unblinkingly. Then without a word she crossed the room, her head regally high, her walk slow, drawing attention to the undulation of her hips.

But Joss kept his gaze on her face, trying to read what lay

behind her calm countenance. For there was *something*. The frisson of energy that charged down his spine when his gaze locked with hers proved it.

He could almost hear the words she wasn't saying.

Almost, but infuriatingly not quite.

He followed her, stopping abruptly as she halted in the doorway.

Her scent invaded his nostrils, not the heavy attar of roses from the wedding, but something light and fresh, barely discernible as he tilted his head towards her neat chignon.

This close he felt it again as he had on the runway yesterday: tension crackling in the air as if she generated some unseen power that magnetised his skin.

What was it about Leila that drew him?

'Which is the small sitting room? You have several.'

'To the right,' he said. 'Third door along.'

Following, Joss allowed his gaze free rein, cataloguing each dip and sway as she moved. His wife didn't flaunt herself with an exaggerated strut. Yet with each slow step the slide of silk over her backside and flaring around her legs screamed 'woman' in a way that had all his attention.

Was his wife sending him an invitation?

The possibility intrigued him. Yet remembering her cool look in the kitchen it didn't seem likely.

Besides, this was a marriage of convenience. She'd be an excellent society hostess and her connections would be invaluable. For her part Leila would acquire prestige, an even more luxurious lifestyle and unprecedented spending power.

A win-win deal. Only a fool would mess with that for the sake of sex. It would complicate everything.

With a wife he couldn't cancel all calls or silence protestations of devotion with an expensive farewell gift. Nor did he intend to face a moody spouse, smarting over some apparent slight, when they hosted an important dinner.

Sex with his wife might raise her expectations of a family one day; though he'd made it clear children weren't on his agenda.

His flesh chilled. No, this arrangement would remain simple. Impersonal.

Yet Joss's gaze didn't shift from Leila as she entered the sitting room and took a seat, the picture of feminine grace. He had the unsettling suspicion he'd got more than he'd bargained for in this marriage of mutual convenience.

Leila chose a deep chair. The soft leather cocooned her and the frisson of disquiet she'd felt since Joss had arrived eased a fraction. She didn't feel ready to deal with him when there was so much else on her mind.

Waking disorientated in an apartment that was all minimalist luxury she'd felt a wave of relief, finding herself alone. No one else had shared the huge bed, and the wardrobe was devoid of Joss's clothes. Yet she'd barely had time to register thankfulness that he'd kept his word and his distance.

Too quickly her thoughts had turned to yesterday's suffocating fear at the airstrip.

It was something she'd never experienced before. When she'd stepped onto the airfield the vastness of the open air had pressed down as if squeezing the life out of her.

Was it something to do with the sudden change after being forcibly kept indoors, confined for long periods?

She could only hope yesterday had been a one-off. She had no intention of letting the past dictate her future.

'Your room is comfortable?' Joss sat, stretching his long legs with the assurance of a man supremely comfortable with their glamorous setting. The place screamed wealth from the stunning views down the Thames, to the original artworks and designer furniture that impressed rather than welcomed.

With his back to the window it was hard to read his expression but she'd bet it was satisfied.

'Very comfortable. Thank you.' Leila had grown up with

wealth, but nothing like this place. And the last few years she'd led a spartan existence, until her stepfather had pulled out all the stops to impress Joss Carmody.

Even the feel of silk against her skin was an unfamiliar sensual delight. As for wearing heels…she'd chosen stilettos today, hoping to get used to the feel of walking on stilts. She intended to take every opportunity to break with the past.

Silence descended. Did her husband have as little idea of what to say to his stranger-spouse as she did?

'Have you lived here long?'

Broad shoulders shrugged. 'I bought the penthouse a couple of years ago but I haven't been here much. I tend to move wherever business takes me.'

She nodded. Mrs Draycott had intimated it was a pleasure having people to look after. Leila understood it was rare for Joss to be on the premises.

That suited her. She'd rather be alone to take her time sorting out her new life.

'How long will you be here?'

His long fingers drummed on the armrest. 'We'll be here at least a month.'

No mistaking the subtle emphasis on the pronoun. Leila's heart skipped a beat. 'We?'

'Of course. We *are* just married, after all.'

Leila pushed aside panic at the thought of sharing even such spacious premises with Joss Carmody. Despite their agreement to pursue separate lives, her hackles rose defensively at the idea of being close to him for even a short time. He was powerful, self-satisfied and used to getting his own way. Characteristics that reminded her too forcefully of Gamil.

Yet she understood Joss wouldn't want to broadcast the fact their marriage was a paper one only. No doubt their separation would be arranged discreetly later.

She'd use the time to investigate her study options and find the perfect home. She longed for a house with a garden, but maybe a flat would be more practical till she found her feet.

But a whole month here? Surely that wouldn't be necessary. Once she had her money—

'Leila?' She looked up to find him staring. 'What is it? You don't like the penthouse?'

'On the contrary, it's very pleasant.'

'Pleasant?' One dark eyebrow shot up. 'I've heard it called many things but not that.'

'I'm sorry if I offended you,' Leila said slowly. 'The apartment is spectacular.' If you enjoyed cold modern minimalism that broadcast too ostentatiously that it cost the earth.

'Here you are, sir, madam.' Mrs Draycott entered with a vast tray. 'There are sandwiches and—' she shot a smiling glance at Leila '—Middle Eastern nut rolls in syrup and cakes flavoured with rosewater. I thought you might appreciate a little reminder of home, madam.'

'Thank you. That's very kind.' Even though memories of home were now fatally tainted.

Leila accepted a plate heaped with delicacies and smiled at the housekeeper as she left the room.

'These are good,' Joss said after polishing off one of the pastries and reaching for a second.

'You have a sweet tooth?' Leila put her plate down on a side table and reached for her tea. 'Did your mother make you sweet treats as a child?' Though they'd always had a cook, Leila remembered her mother's occasional baking as the best in the world.

'No.' The word seemed shorter than ever in that brusque tone. 'My mother didn't sully her hands with anything as mundane as cooking.'

'I see.' His tone didn't encourage further comment.

'I doubt it.' Joss's voice was cool but the fierce angle of his pinched eyebrows told of harnessed emotions.

'My mother abhorred anything that might interfere with

her girlish figure or delicate hands.' His gazed raked her and
Leila's skin prickled as if he'd touched her. 'Plus she believed
the world revolved around her. She had no inclination for anything *domestic* if it involved dirtying her hands. That's what
other people were for.'

Leila frowned at his scathing assessment. Or perhaps it
was the burn of ice-cold fury in his eyes.

She looked away, uncomfortable with the sudden seismic
emotion surging beneath his composure.

They were strangers and she'd prefer they stayed that way.
The trembling hint of sympathy she felt at what sounded like
an uncomfortable home life wasn't something she wanted
to pursue.

Instinctively she knew he wouldn't thank her for it.

Leila cast around for a response. 'Your mother must be
very impressed at all this.' Her gesture took in the architect-
designed penthouse in a building that was the last word in
London exclusivity.

And maybe that explained the soulless feel of the place.
Apparently Joss didn't have the time or inclination for anything as domestic as furnishing his home. This looked as if
it had been decorated by a very chic, very talented designer
who wanted to make a bold statement rather than a home.

'My mother isn't alive.' Joss's gaze grew hooded as he let
the silence between them grow. 'I don't have a family.'

'I'm sorry.'

'The absence of relatives at the wedding didn't alert you?'
His tone was abrupt and Leila cursed herself for not notic-
ing. Given the number of Gamil's invitees, the imbalance
should have been glaringly obvious. Except she'd been on
tenterhooks wondering if she'd finally managed to escape his
clutches. Most of the day had been a blur of fear and elation.

'No. I...'

Her words petered out in face of Joss's frown. From his

steely expression it was clear he considered her abominably self-absorbed.

'Nor do I want a family. I have no interest in continuing the family name.' His eyes bored into her, their intense glitter pinioning her. 'And I don't see any point bringing more children into a world that can't feed the mouths we've already got.'

He looked pointedly at her plate, still laden with Mrs Draycott's carefully prepared treats.

Leila's stomach cramped at the thought of all that intense cloying sweetness. After her recent meagre rations she hadn't a hope of eating all this rich food. That had to be part of the reason she'd felt unwell yesterday, trying to force down the elaborate wedding feast under Gamil's watchful glare.

But, short of revealing to Joss the real reason for her lack of appetite, there was nothing she could do but eat. Joss might not be cast in the same mould as Gamil but she'd take no chances. He was bossy, powerful and authoritarian. She'd learned to her cost that domineering men couldn't be trusted. There was no way she'd trust Joss with the story of Gamil's brutality and her own helplessness against him. Who knew how he might use that against her?

Besides, the memory filled her with shame. Logic told her she'd done all she could to withstand Gamil's abuse, but part of her cried out in self-disgust at the fact she'd been a victim.

Reluctantly she reached for a tiny cake. Inhaling its rich honeyed scent, she felt a wave of nausea hit her and she hesitated.

'I happen to know Mrs Draycott went to a lot of effort to make something special for you.'

Leila felt the weight of Joss's scrutiny as she bit into the delicacy.

Bittersweet memories drenched her with that first taste. Of a time when she'd taken happiness for granted. Her mother laughing in their Paris kitchen with their cook's enormous apron wrapped twice around her slim form. Leila's father, debonair in evening jacket, sneaking a cake from a cooling rack and having his hand smacked, so he wreaked his revenge with a loud kiss on his wife's lips. Memories of childhood birthday parties and smiles.

'It's good,' Leila murmured and risked another bite.

Too soon the memories were dislodged as bile rose in her throat. Her stomach churned in a sickening mix of distress and unsatisfied hunger.

She made to rise. 'Excuse me, I need—'

'The bathroom?' Joss's tone was rusty with anger and she swung her head up to find him scowling down at her. 'Why? So you can dislodge any trace of food from your system?'

Leila shook her head, stunned by his anger.

'I'm feeling a little unwell, that's all. I—'

'You're making yourself unwell, don't you mean?'

'No!' She surged to her feet. 'I don't mean that at all.' She was tired of having people put words into her mouth and over-seeing her every move. She was weary and out of sorts and—

'Tell me, Leila.' His voice was lethally quiet as he stalked across to block her exit. 'Is it bulimia or anorexia?'

Joss was determined to sort this out *now*.

His fragile patience for pampered princesses grew threadbare. And somewhere, deep inside, was a thread of real fear, the knowledge of precisely how dangerous an eating disorder was.

It did no good to tell himself Leila wasn't his concern. He couldn't turn his back.

'It's neither!' Her head reared back in what looked like genuine shock. 'There's nothing wrong with my eating habits.'

He surveyed her slowly, pleased to see her sick pallor had abated, replaced by spots of high colour in her cheeks and fire in her eyes.

It struck him that his wife was beautiful when roused.

'Then why have I never seen you consume more than a bite? Why are you sick after eating?'

He stepped nearer, close enough to inhale her fresh scent, and she angled her head high. He'd give her this: she didn't back down from confrontation. His skin sizzled as she surveyed him. A pulse of something like desire beat hard in his belly.

If he'd known Leila could be so…animated, he might have thought twice about marriage. He'd wanted a demure, stylish hostess, not a spitfire. But the coiling heat in his lower body made a lie of the thought.

'Do you always jump to conclusions?' One fine eyebrow arched high on her smooth forehead, giving her a supercilious, touch-me-not air that made him want to level the barriers between them and give her a taste of raw, earthy pleasure. The force of that need shocked him.

'Do you always avoid questions for which you've no answer?'

Her nostrils flared as if she kept tight rein on a quick temper. Unbidden, interest stirred. He'd always liked passion in a woman—in bed, not emotionally.

The thought brought him up sharply.

Leila was his *wife*. He was not going to bed her. He was not going to risk the possibility of messy, emotional scenes with the woman he'd just tied himself to.

She folded her hands in a show of patience that might have fooled him but for the heat still simmering in those luminous eyes. Despite his better judgement he found himself enjoying the contrast.

'I haven't been eating rich meals lately. The food at the wedding feast was designed to impress but it wasn't to my taste.'

'You've been dieting? Didn't your father warn you about becoming underweight?' His mouth thinned at her stupidity. Didn't she value her health?

'*Step*father.' Instantly she pursed her lips as if regretting the correction. 'And no, he didn't have a problem with my diet.'

Again that puzzling flicker of almost-expression crossed her face, as if she suppressed something. Something Joss was determined to uncover.

'And now? You can't tell me the cakes aren't to your taste. I saw the look on your face when you took that first bite.' She'd closed her eyes as if overcome by bliss. The sight of such unadulterated sensual pleasure had been arresting, drawing him towards her and heating a coil of masculine anticipation low in his groin.

Leila shrugged. 'It was lovely but, as I said, my diet has been very plain, very…restricted. This was just too much of a good thing.'

Joss clamped down the surge of admonition on his tongue. He knew she hid something. But her shock at his accusation seemed genuine. For the moment he'd have to reserve judgement.

'And now? Do you still feel sick?'

She tilted her head, her eyes widening. 'You know…' she paused as if considering '…I don't!' She looked genuinely pleased.

'Good. You need to build up your appetite.'

'I do?'

He nodded, already resuming his seat and picking up his coffee. He was savvy enough to realise it would take a while to get to the bottom of whatever ailed Leila. 'I'm going away on business but when I return and we start entertaining you won't be able to run to the bathroom through every meal.'

Entertaining? Shock slammed her and her stomach knotted in dismay. Since when would a couple leading separate lives entertain guests?

Leila sank into her chair, her eyes fixed on Joss as he

drained his coffee then bit into another syrupy nut roll with strong white teeth. Dazed, she watched the rhythmic movement of his solid jaw. Clearly he was a man of healthy appetite, part of her brain registered, just as if she weren't reeling from his announcement.

'What do you mean, entertaining?'

'You'll assist when we have guests.' He shrugged. 'A lot of business is done, connections made, socially. One of the reasons I considered you a suitable bride is your pedigree: child of diplomats, brought up in the best circles, with links to many powerful families with whom I'll be doing business.' He sat back, clearly pleased with himself. 'You're a born hostess. It was one of the things I checked when we met.'

'Indeed.' The word emerged between gritted teeth. Her skin prickled as fury engulfed her.

He looked so smug that he'd deigned to *consider her suitable* as his wife. And he wanted her to be his hostess? As if *she* owed *him* something! He'd come to *her*, wanting her inheritance.

'That wasn't in our agreement,' she bit out.

'It wasn't?' His sculpted lower lip firmed. His eyes narrowed and abruptly the tension in the air thickened.

'No.' Leila refused to be cowed. 'You didn't mention us entertaining together.'

Slowly Joss crossed one leg over another. His fingers splayed over the arms of his chair. But Leila wasn't fooled into believing he was relaxed. There was an alertness about him that made her think of a predator, sizing up dinner.

'You think the mere fact of our marriage entitles you to be kept in the style to which you'd like to be accustomed? Without stirring yourself in any way?'

'You're a fine one to talk. You married me for my father's oil-rich land.' How dared he try to make her sound mercenary?

'So I did.' His smile had a hungry edge that tightened

every nerve. 'And in doing so I acquired a hostess to help me achieve my goals. At present that involves smoothing my dealings with the elite of European and Middle Eastern society. You're perfectly placed to assist me.'

Perfectly placed!

Leila pressed her lips together rather than let rip with a scathing retort.

'I'm afraid I have other plans.' She sat back and stared into sparking midnight-dark eyes.

She was safe now, out of Bakhara. Soon she'd have her own funds and in a country like England Joss couldn't impose his will as her stepfather had.

'Other plans?' Joss surveyed her critically, noting the mulish line of her lips. 'How can you have other plans when we've just married?'

He stifled a sigh. Wasn't this one of the reasons he'd avoided marriage? The contrariness of women? To marry and then tell him she had *other plans*!

If she thought to play him the way his mother had played everyone around her, Leila had plenty to learn.

Leila shrugged and her insouciance needled a spur of annoyance under his skin. 'You said this was a paper marriage. You made it clear we'd live separate lives.'

Why did her eagerness to be rid of him rankle? He didn't want a clinging vine. But he wasn't used to a woman trying to dump him. *He* always ended relationships.

'So we will. Except when we appear together for major social functions.' He knew her interest in his dividends. She'd sold herself without any pretence of emotional connection. That had been the clinching factor in his decision to marry her.

'Don't worry, I won't interfere in your private life so long as you're discreet.' He smiled, secure in the knowledge the penalty clause for pregnancy in their prenup meant she wouldn't try foisting another man's baby on him. 'But there *will* be times when I need your services as hostess.'

'And if I refuse?' Her voice was cool.

'Refuse?' The idea of anyone refusing Joss was so novel it took a moment for anger to kick in. 'Don't be absurd. Why would you refuse?' Surely she wasn't so lazy as to begrudge this small effort?

'It doesn't suit me. I intend to live my own life from now on.'

Joss fixed her with a glare. 'I think not, dear wife.' His words were silky, delivered in a tone under-performing managers on four continents dreaded. 'Remember the prenup you signed. You've already agreed to this. You have no choice.'

CHAPTER FOUR

THE AIR SQUEEZED from Leila's chest.

He wasn't kidding.

What sort of man specified such detail in a marriage agreement? Weren't they supposed to be about safeguarding wealth, not setting out wifely duties?

Though looking into his furious eyes, Leila realised Joss Carmody was the sort of man who crossed every t and dotted every i, especially in business. And this marriage was business.

Leila clung to that like a lifeline in a stormy sea. Business she could cope with, it was emotional games she couldn't face.

'You did *read* the prenup?' One ebony eyebrow shot up in disbelief.

How she hated his supercilious expression! She'd had enough of men who thought themselves superior.

Leila's hands curled into damp palms, her nails scoring her flesh.

She'd wanted to read the papers but her stepfather had covered them so all she'd seen was the bottom of each page where she'd initialled and the final page where she'd signed in full. She'd been furious and frustrated, but so desperate she'd signed. It had made her sick to the stomach but she'd forced herself to do it so she could get away.

'Leila?' Joss's terse voice demanded an instant response.

Had she escaped one tyrant only to fall under the yoke of another? Her heart plummeted at the possibility.

'I must have skimmed that section.'

Pride demanded she gloss over the truth. That was in the past. She refused to revisit it, especially in front of a man who viewed her as a tool to be used for his own ends.

Her stepfather had exploited any weakness. Leila had no intention of revealing weakness to any man again. Especially to her husband. *It was too dangerous.*

Dark eyes bored into hers. It felt like a daring luxury to meet his stare head-on and not look away as she'd trained herself to do with Gamil. Even something as small as that made her feel strong and intrepid.

How far her stepfather had eroded her life!

Leila was determined to start anew as she meant to go on. Now she was free, or almost, she'd never let a man bully her again.

'Ah, you concentrated on the financial rewards. Naturally.' Joss nodded. He didn't even sound sarcastic. He seriously believed money was all she cared about.

'You don't think much of women, do you?'

He looked surprised. 'I treat people as I find them, male or female.'

Which meant he had little respect for anyone.

What sort of man had she married? She knew of his ruthless reputation in business—that was something Gamil respected. But she'd assumed Joss would have a softer side, not with her, but with *someone*.

She pushed aside the memory of the competent way he'd handled her weakness yesterday. His unfussy sympathy that had eased her fear.

He'd dealt with the situation because he'd had to get to London. That was all there was to it. She'd be foolish to mistake necessity for caring.

Everything she learned about him confirmed he was a man she preferred not to know better.

'So the contract specifies my duties as hostess.' Leila forced her mind to the matter in hand. 'Is there anything else?' She was proud of the cool tone that hid galloping nerves. What else was included in those papers?

'I'll have a copy brought round so you can reacquaint yourself with it.' He shot a look at his custom-made watch, as if turning his mind to more important matters.

Damn him! *This* was important.

'Indulge me, Joss.' She crossed her legs and eased back nonchalantly though every tensed muscle protested. Instinctively she hid how desperate she was for details.

His gaze returned, travelling the length of her legs before skimming her dress to rest on her face. Leila's skin tingled where his look brushed her like a caress. Defiantly she angled her chin, pretending she felt nothing.

Something flickered in his hooded eyes. Her nape prickled as if she confronted danger.

Clearly Joss was used to calling the shots, not answering questions.

Strange how the flare of warning in his eyes spurred her on. As if she enjoyed her ability to provoke him. After years of feigned subservience it was wonderful to exercise her independence even in such a small way.

She stroked her mother's pearl pendant, projecting an air of casual interest. 'What else might I have missed?'

His stillness was unnerving. He was so completely focused on her, and, it appeared, on the massive pearl in her hand. Hurriedly she released the pendant, feeling it fall between her breasts.

Joss's eyes fixed on the spot where it rested and Leila's breath hissed in a rush of reaction as heat hazed her breasts and her pulse danced.

She wasn't used to being looked at like that.

'You should read the papers.' His tone suggested she wouldn't understand them. Annoyance shook her from the strange stasis his look had induced.

'I will.' Leila made her smile saccharine sweet. 'But in the meantime…?'

He exhaled audibly, his jaw tensing—an indication he wasn't totally in control. Her smile widened. She detested the idea he could simply dismiss her as his latest commercial acquisition.

'You agreed to act as my hostess, but don't worry, the work won't be hard. There'll be plenty of time for…' He waved a hand as if unsure what ordinary people did with their time.

'Shopping?' Her smile grew fixed. Her stepfather's obsessive need to control had deprived her of the right to make even the smallest decisions. Now she'd married a man who thought she wanted only to spend his money! It didn't occur to him that she might aspire to a career.

'Precisely.' He gestured again. 'Apart from that there are penalties if you embroil yourself in scandal. Penalties for divorce or pregnancy—'

'Penalties for *what*?' Her tone rose in disbelief.

'You heard me.' He drained his coffee as casually as if they discussed the weather. 'I specified no children in this marriage.'

'I remember.' How could she forget? She'd clung to the knowledge he didn't expect her to share his bed. 'But surely it takes two to—'

'It may very well take two to conceive a child but I won't be one of them.' The words shot out like rifle fire, biting into her. The warning glitter in his eyes chilled her to the marrow.

Finally she understood. He meant children with other men, other lovers.

'If you find yourself pregnant, don't come whining to me for support. You'd lose every benefit this marriage gives you.'

His tone was glacial, each syllable brittle with disdain. He looked every inch the tycoon, a man devoid of human warmth.

'Don't look so shocked, Leila. I'm sure you're too sensible to get pregnant.'

His distaste was unmistakeable. For the notion of a child? Or at the idea of getting her pregnant himself? It couldn't be at the possibility of his wife having sex with another man. Joss had told her she could do as she liked so long as she was 'discreet'. He virtually invited her to sleep around, so long as she didn't become pregnant!

Leila had experienced degradation at her stepfather's hands but Joss plumbed new depths. He'd managed to hurt a part of her Gamil had never touched. Pain scored her vitals and she sat straighter, every sinew taut with disgust.

This shouldn't hurt. She knew Joss had a low opinion of her. Yet his casual assumption about her morals felt like the final straw.

'Don't worry. I won't get pregnant.' When she eventually had children it would be with a man she loved. A man who loved her with his whole being, not a man fixated on contracts and profits. One day when this union was just a bad memory...

Her forced smile felt stiff but Joss's narrowed eyes told her it looked real. It prompted her to make her point.

'I have no intention of sleeping with any man, especially you.'

Joss put his cup down on the table with a precise click, his gaze fixed on her. 'Oh,' he murmured, his voice a low purr that fuzzed the sensitive skin of her neck and arms, 'I never *sleep* with women. My interest in them is rather more active than that. I always sleep alone.'

His lips curled in a smile of pure satisfaction that sent a warning jangling through her. Despite his despicably smug attitude, that smile was *dangerous*.

Fire seared Leila's face as he did that thing with his eyes, that sweeping glance that drew every nerve tight with thrumming awareness.

Whatever this strange sensation was she'd almost rather face the sick panic she'd experienced at the airport yesterday. Instinct warned her that the unfamiliar awareness deep inside put her at Joss's mercy.

Leila couldn't allow that to happen.

She'd be at no man's mercy ever again.

Deliberately she shifted her weight, settling more squarely in the seat and recrossing her legs, projecting an air of assurance. She lifted the pendant, reassured by its smooth solidity and the fact it had been her mother's. Gamil had kept it and the rest of her mother's jewellery locked away, begrudgingly giving this to her so she could dress the part to convince Joss she was a suitable fiancée.

'Excellent.' She paused to make sure she had Joss's full attention. 'It's reassuring to hear confirmation you don't expect intimacy.' She pitched her voice low. 'Just make sure you maintain your *fitness* regime elsewhere. Accidental meetings with your workout partners would be so tiresome.'

Joss's eyes widened fractionally, and then to her amazement he tipped his head back and laughed.

The sound was deep and rich, surprisingly inviting. Amusement cast his features in a younger, more approachable light. Yet she felt no inclination to join his mirth.

'Touché. Spoken like a true wife.'

'I'll do better next time,' she bit, annoyed at being the butt of his humour.

At his quizzical look she explained, 'It's not a real wife you want.'

'Of course not.'

The laugh died on Joss's lips. For an instant there, enjoying her sharp retort, he'd almost forgotten the need for distance between them. Getting close to his wife would complicate things unnecessarily.

He preferred curvaceous, accommodating blondes. Not underfed, sharp-tongued brunettes who questioned and prodded.

Yet heat danced in his belly as he watched her chin notch higher and her eyes flash emerald fire. The pendant throbbed with her every breath, drawing his gaze again to that demure bodice, which did such a poor job of concealing her firm, high breasts. Thank God she hadn't dieted hard enough to be skin and bone there.

Those breasts had pressed against him as he'd carried her, reminding him that despite what their contract said his wife was all woman.

'And if I decline to act as your hostess?' Her question ambushed him as he lingered over thoughts of how Leila's breasts would look minus the beige silk.

'Why would you?' He sat forward a fraction, intrigued despite himself. Why did she make so much of such a small thing, coming back to it yet again?

Most women would love helping him host exclusive parties or being escorted to A-list events.

Leila shrugged and played with her bracelet, exuding an air of nonchalance that almost fooled him, till he saw her other hand locked in a tight fist. Curiosity deepened.

'It's the one thing I want from you.' Apart from the land he'd secured. 'If you don't honour our agreement, I'll sever it. You'll return to Bakhara immediately.'

Her breath hissed. Stormy eyes clashed with his. He read emotion there, strong emotion. Then there was a clattering sound and she tore her gaze away, long lashes veiling her eyes.

Around her feet precious black pearls bounced and rolled. Yet Leila sat as if frozen, one hand fisted in her lap and the other grasping the broken catch of her bracelet so hard it shook.

'Leila?' Joss half rose to go to her, till he realised what he was doing and subsided.

She didn't notice, her gaze was fixed on the floor.

'Leila, what is it?'

Damn it! She infuriated him. One moment she was sassy and challenging and the next... He couldn't put his finger on it but the word 'vulnerable' came to mind.

Hah! She was as vulnerable as an icebreaker, cruising through life. Witness her casual attitude to reading important legal documents. She was used to stepdaddy looking out for her and no doubt bailing her out financially.

Leila had grown up with all the advantages of wealth. Gamil said she'd even finished her education privately rather than trouble herself attending classes with the hoi polloi.

'I don't know my own strength.' She gestured to the pearls spinning on the high-gloss wood floor. Her lips curved in a familiar cool smile that this time wasn't convincing.

To his amazement Joss realised her husky tone revealed stress. This wasn't a game after all. But what was it?

She shuffled forward in her seat as if to go down on her knees and collect the pearls.

'You don't want to go home?'

Instantly she stilled. She shrugged but tellingly didn't meet his eyes. 'I've lived all over the world. Bakhara isn't necessarily home.'

Did she think he hadn't noticed her evasion?

Did she take him for a fool?

He reminded himself it didn't matter what Leila's personal hang-ups were, so long as she fulfilled their bargain. He had more pressing matters to attend to. But he found himself persisting.

'You didn't answer me, Leila. Why don't you want to return to Bakhara?'

Her shoulders hunched high, her hands clenching in her lap. Then with a deep breath she deliberately opened her hands and placed them on the wide arms of her chair, sinking back as if at ease. She looked the epitome of relaxed nonchalance. Almost.

Joss could read people. In Leila he found a challenge, a woman who hid more than she revealed. But he saw tension cloak every line of her slim form.

'I've lived there for years. It's time for a change. I'm used to moving every few years.'

She waved a hand airily and a mark caught his eye. A bluish line ringing her slender arm. The double row of massive pearls at her wrist had concealed it today, and yesterday a fortune in gold bangles had hidden the spot. The intricate henna decoration on her hands and wrists obscured it, but the underside of her arm was definitely marked, and not in henna.

It was an encircling bruise.

Tension churned deep in his belly and with it sickening doubt.

He recalled the way she'd looked over her shoulder the day they'd first met, as if worried someone would overhear or seeking cues from a hidden bystander. He'd been so intent on pushing through the deal he hadn't bothered to consider what it meant. Now he did and the possibilities hollowed his gut.

Guilt, an emotion he barely remembered, surfaced.

Had she been coerced into marrying him?

Leila reeled from the discovery she was trapped. Horror filled her.

Gamil had already bragged of stealing the money her parents had left her. 'Investing' it, he'd said. Investing it in his own schemes for self-promotion! Without her money Leila had relied on the allowance she'd get from marriage to fund her independence.

Except that allowance was tied to her living with Joss! Unless she wanted to be packed off back to her stepfather.

She shuddered as her dreams crumbled around her. She'd do *anything* to avoid going back.

Joss surged to his feet. The violence of his movement made her flinch, the tang of fear sharp on her tongue, till she conquered the response instilled by years with Gamil and forced her muscles to relax.

Warily she looked up.

Joss didn't approach but stalked to the windows, tall and imposing against the late-afternoon light. She watched, fascinated by the restrained energy of his long-legged stride.

He looked as if he should be out conquering mountains or striding the deck of an oil rig, the wind in his hair and his eyes narrowed against the harsh sun. He was dynamic and strong. Even his business clothes couldn't hide the breadth of those shoulders or the power in his thighs.

Joss had a potent, masculine air of purpose she'd never seen in any man. Or was it just that she'd been cloistered too long? His sheer magnetism drew her gaze and did strange things to her insides.

She remembered him carrying her. How wonderfully secure she'd felt for the first time in years. She'd had to remind herself security came from independence, not a solid chest and strong arms.

'Tell me.' He swung round abruptly, his voice harsh. 'Were you forced into this marriage?'

Leila's eyes widened.

'Answer me!' His voice was terse, his stance rigid. Then, as if realising he'd barked the command, his tone softened. 'Leila?'

Stunned, she shook her head. 'Would you care if I was?' He'd wanted the marriage and what Joss Carmody wanted he got. Her agreement was a mere formality to the arrangements agreed between him and Gamil. That still galled her. She was sick of being manipulated.

'It's true, then?' Even with the light behind him, Leila saw

he looked shaken. Gone was the expression of complete confidence. His strong features were stark with shock.

'No.' Annoyed though she was, Leila couldn't lie. 'It's
not true.'

Joss took a stride towards her then stopped, lifting his hand
to rub the back of his neck. For the first time since they'd met
he looked uncertain.

'You can tell me if your stepfather forced you into marriage.' There was a note in his voice that sounded like sympathy, despite its gruff edge.

'What makes you think he did?' Leila blinked, wondering what she'd said to make him think so. Determined to put
the past behind her, and with her expertise in concealing her
thoughts, she couldn't believe she'd revealed Gamil's hold
over her.

Joss paced closer, heedless of the pearls skidding from his
polished shoes. He reached out and took her hand, his long
fingers firm and warm against her flesh.

Fine wires of heat spun through her veins and drew her
skin tight. Leila had never known anything like the gossamer
net of warmth raying from his touch.

She tugged but instead of releasing her he turned her hand
over.

There, on the pale underside of her arm, she saw telling
marks. The imprint of Gamil's fingers.

It was rare for Gamil to touch her. If anything he'd always
seemed to dislike physical contact. But his anger had reached
fever pitch at what he had deemed Leila's insolence. Gamil
had grabbed her while he spat his fury at her.

Shivering, she thrust the memory aside, focusing on the
present. On her wrist. On the way Joss's bronzed hand cradled hers so gently.

The sight brought a skewed smile to her lips.

How long since she'd known gentleness?

Hard on the thought came the realisation it could be a ruse.

Her stepfather had been a master at mind games; waiting till the precise moment she was most vulnerable to wreak vengeance for supposed misdemeanours.

Was Joss luring her into dropping her defences?

A tiny protest rose—that Joss, for all his faults, wasn't Gamil. But how could she be sure? She didn't want to put it to the test.

'Leila?' His voice was low.

Slowly she raised her head to find he'd bent close. Those dark eyes remained unreadable yet his look sent warmth shuddering through her.

'Gamil got agitated about something and held me too tightly.' Pride, the need to keep her past weakness hidden, prevented her revealing what Gamil had done. The last thing she needed was for her new husband to learn she could be cowed and browbeaten. Even though she assured herself that here in Britain even a husband didn't have the power over her that her guardian had wielded in Bakhara.

'Did he hurt you often?' Joss's voice was a soft growl. His fingers tightened. Not painfully, but…supportively.

It felt so real. But was it?

Confusion filled her. The desire to trust warring with caution learned at the mercy of a vicious, dangerous brute.

Leila looked away. 'This is the only time he bruised me. It's not his way.' She drew a deep breath, knowing she should pull back but unable to sever the contact. The only friendly touch she'd known since her mother died was Joss's. It was all she could do not to curl her fingers around his and beg him to hold her as he had yesterday.

The wayward thought horrified her. How easily he breached her defences!

'I wasn't forced into marriage.' Leila kept her gaze on their hands. Hers slender and feminine with its temporary henna patterns of flowers and birds. His sinewy and squarish, with fingers long enough to wrap around her wrist. 'I agreed to the wedding. There was no coercion.'

Strange how those words sounded different when her hand rested in his. She was so *aware* of him, the spicy scent of his skin, his breath grazing her face, his frame, taller and broader, less than an arm's length away.

Would she react like this to any man?

'You're sure? Now is the time to tell me.'

'It's true. I *wanted* to marry you.' How could she not? Anything was preferable to the life she'd led.

'I'm pleased to hear it.'

Joss lifted her hand. Her gaze rose till she met eyes of deepest indigo.

To her amazement he lifted her hand to his mouth, his lips grazing a whisper-soft caress against her skin.

Leila's eyes widened. She'd never been kissed before. The contact sent sensation zinging through her. Dazedly she wondered how a kiss on the mouth felt.

As she watched Joss pressed his lips to the sensitive skin of her wrist, right over the fading bruise.

Leila's breath escaped in a whoosh of air. His lips caressed in a way that made her shiver as sensations she'd never known ran riot through her body. Her mouth dried and her nipples drew tight and hard.

Joss Carmody was dangerous. One touch, just a hint of gentleness, and she was completely out of her depth.

CHAPTER FIVE

HELL! WHAT HAD got into him?

Joss had been away almost two weeks, dealing with an oil-rig fire and its aftermath in the Timor Sea. Days of crisis management and too little sleep. Yet his thoughts had strayed continually to Leila. *His wife.* To the taste of her soft skin, the promise of delight in her dazed eyes and parted lips. To that hint of vulnerability, quickly hidden.

Since when had any woman created such havoc?

She was a business asset, no more. Acquired in a deal that allowed him the challenge of new enterprises—drilling for oil as well as developing the perfect site for a radical alternative power plant. The Sheikh of Bakhara himself was interested in that scheme, if Joss could bring it together.

Leila was a means to an end.

So why did she invade his thoughts when he should have been snatching precious sleep or, worse, when he was working?

Had this marriage been an error of judgement?

Joss didn't make errors of judgement. He sized up each situation, determined what needed to be done, then followed through: swiftly, effectively and unemotionally.

But this marriage of convenience wasn't as convenient as he'd thought.

Leila distracted him from his goals. Why this consuming curiosity to know more about her?

She evoked protective instincts he hadn't experienced since Joanna had succumbed to an illness that no one, least of all a ten-year-old brother, had been able to stop.

Joss told himself that was why Leila had snagged his interest. She roused fears of the same happening to her.

But it was more than that.

With her tantalising anomalies, contradictory hauteur and vulnerability, Leila disturbed his equilibrium. He told himself no one as grounded as she could be anorexic, but she'd definitely been far too thin. She was feisty yet reserved. She was bright but she hadn't bothered to read their prenup. Above all she was secretive.

Perhaps that was it. He didn't like not knowing what was going on. Once he understood her he could put her from his mind.

Soon, he hoped! He'd been back in London only a few hours, in the apartment just long enough to shower and change, and already he was eager to see her.

Joss wrenched off his bow tie and threw it down, annoyed that anticipation prickled his spine at the thought of seeing Leila again.

He grabbed a fresh tie and looped it round his neck, tying a perfect bow. His mouth twisted. His mother would have approved. She'd set such store by appearances. Wrangling formal dress was something he'd learned almost in infancy. His father, on the other hand, had taught him to look beyond the surface. To learn a man's weakness…and exploit it.

Joss grimaced at his reflection in the mirror. He'd rather do business in a boardroom or an outback shed than at a society party, but needs must.

He strode from the room.

Leila was waiting in the larger sitting room. The sight of her slammed him to a stop.

'What are you wearing?' Disbelief turned the question into a bark of accusation.

Slowly she turned from examining a modern sculpture. He had time to note the steel in her spine as well as the delicacy of her slender frame. At least she didn't look quite so underweight now.

Relief eased his muscles. He told himself it was purely impersonal. He needed her healthy enough to be at his side on demand. That was why he'd instructed Mrs Draycott to ensure Leila ate in his absence.

'Clearly that's a rhetorical question. Unless something has happened to your eyesight?'

The colour in her cheeks and the flash of temper in her eyes almost distracted him from the catastrophe of her clothes. They hinted that behind her poise and superior air lurked a woman of fire and passion, which piqued all sorts of inappropriate thoughts.

That annoyed him even more than what she'd chosen to wear for their first public appearance. Did she want to make a laughing-stock of him?

'Poor eyesight would be preferable.' He shook his head in disgust. 'What possessed you? I want my wife looking glamorous, not like a bag lady.'

Leila lifted her chin high in a move he realised now was characteristic. It bared her long, delicate throat and made him want to reach out and see if the flesh there was as exquisitely fine as it appeared.

'It's from a leading couture house.' Her eyes snapped but her voice was calm. 'I doubt they get many bag ladies.'

'I don't care where it's from.' Joss took in the fussy design that concealed her natural assets. 'That navy makes you look washed out and it hangs like a sack.' He shook his head, appalled. 'Take it off. Now!'

For a horrified moment Leila could only stare up into his dark scowl. Surely he didn't want her to strip for him?

Belatedly logic seeped into her brain and she drew a shaky

breath. That fire in Joss's eyes made her imagine the stupidest things. As if he'd want to see her naked!

She ignored as impossible the tiny splinter of disappointment that grazed her.

The shameful truth was that she was completely off balance. All because she feared she'd give herself away when the time came to leave the apartment. Every day she tried to go out, till a wave of panic engulfed her and sent her reeling, her head spinning and stomach heaving.

She had to get control of herself for her own sanity! She refused to be a prisoner in this plush apartment as she'd been Gamil's prisoner for so long. It was no consolation realising it was probably his maltreatment, the way he'd locked her up, that created her fear.

She was determined to conquer it. But she didn't want Joss witnessing her struggle.

'You want me to change?'

'Got it in one.' His laconic words sounded patronising to her sensitive ears, stiffening her spine. 'Something with colour. Something eye-catching.'

Leila doubted there was anything like that in her vast walk-in robe. She'd had no say in the clothes bought for her trousseau. Her only involvement had been to stand while her measurements were taken. But even that had been a pointless exercise as whoever had ordered the new wardrobe had chosen clothes a size too large.

Gamil's obsession with counteracting her supposedly loose morals and flawed character had obviously influenced the selection. Or was he just having the last laugh?

'Some time soon would be good.'

Leila jerked her head up to find Joss, arms crossed, looking the picture of masculine impatience. The fact that he looked gorgeous—if you liked bold, powerful features and raw testosterone—didn't help.

Her hackles rose. She was *not* his servant to be ordered

around. She'd spent too long dancing to her stepfather's tune to do it again. Indignation was a welcome change from anxiety and the self-doubt that dogged her.

'You're *so* persuasive when you ask nicely, Joss.' She purred his name coolly, putting one hand on her hip in a show of easy confidence. 'I bet women just queue up to get a taste of that charm.'

He didn't move an inch yet suddenly loomed larger than ever. His long fingers twitched then curled at his sides. His midnight eyes glittered and a sizzle shot down her spine that she felt all the way to her toes.

She refused to be cowed. His fury spurred her defiance.

Leila had grown up around men in formal clothes. She'd been a diplomat's daughter. Yet she couldn't remember one to match Joss for sheer impact. Magnificent tailoring complemented what she guessed was an equally magnificent body. But it was his potent power, the sense of barely restrained masculinity, that had shackled her attention from the moment he entered the room.

That and his anger.

Strange how it didn't scare her the way Gamil's cold fury had. But then her stepfather's emotions had been sickly distorted.

By comparison there was something almost reassuringly healthy about the simmering heat in her husband's expression.

Was that why she enjoyed provoking him?

'I'll go change.' She swung towards the door, appalled at her thoughts.

Nevertheless she rather enjoyed the undulating sway her high heels gave her. It made her feel feminine and…powerful. Something she hadn't felt in a long time.

Heat seared her. It should be impossible yet she was sure it was from the impact of his eyes on her. Leila felt his gaze as if he reached out and touched her. The sway of her hips

grew a touch more pronounced. She half turned her head.
'Formal, you said?'

'Formal,' he reiterated. 'I want you to look spectacular.'

Spectacular!

Leila's footsteps faltered and she almost tripped. She
hadn't a hope of achieving spectacular. Even on a good day
and in the loveliest of clothes.

It had taken hours of practice and multiple mistakes just to
get her make-up passable. It had been years since she'd worn
any and it had been no mean feat to replicate the work of the
beautician brought in for the wedding.

Nevertheless Leila held her shoulders straight, determined
not to let Joss see her doubts.

'I'll be back soon.'

Two minutes later Leila surveyed the racks of exquisitely
made clothes her stepfather had ordered. Apart from a couple
of casual dresses and a pair of black trousers that, miracu-
lously, fitted like a glove, the rest was a disaster.

Beige, navy, drab olive and a mustard that made her look
jaundiced. The worst colours for her. Leila flicked through
the clothes, spirits plummeting.

There was nothing spectacular. The best she could hope
for was neat and not over-sized.

With one fluid movement she unzipped the navy dress,
stepped out and hung it up. Then, hands on hips, stood pondering, hoping for inspiration. None came.

'Can't decide?'

The deep drawl from the doorway made her spin round,
her heart thudding high in her throat.

'You can't come in here!' Frantically she searched for a
wrap to throw round herself but everything was stowed away.

She raised her hands to cover herself, till she saw the quizzical tilt of one straight eyebrow and read the glint in his eye.
Heat shimmered under her skin. Her mouth dried and she

was sure the blush covered her whole body. Yet she forced her hands to her sides.

Instinct told her revealing her nerves at being half naked would give Joss a weapon to use against her later. That was how dominating men operated.

He'd see more on a beach any day, she assured herself. Her cream panties and bra were conservatively cut, plus she wore sheer stay-up stockings and stilettos. Yet she felt vulnerable. Whether from baring so much flesh after years of being covered or from the fact it was Joss who saw her, she didn't want to investigate.

Insouciance was beyond her. She settled for keeping her hands at her sides though it strained every muscle to breaking point.

'I can't come in?' He shook his head. 'But I just did.' He paced further into the room she'd once thought enormous. His presence filled it, drawing out all the air and leaving in its place prickling, static electricity. His subtle scent surrounded her.

And his eyes didn't leave her. Surely she imagined heat flaring in those dark irises?

Finally, thankfully, he turned to the clothes on the hangers. Leila put a hand to her chest as she gulped in air and her blood started to pump again.

He rifled through the first few outfits.

'Tell me you didn't choose this stuff.' Disbelief dripped from each word.

'I didn't.'

He didn't turn to face her. 'Then who—'

'My stepfather. It's complicated.'

Joss paused, then began shoving his way through the hangers again. Clearly he had no interest in the reasons for her sombre wardrobe. All he cared about was her appearance as a fitting companion. She had a precise function in his life and that was all that concerned him.

It should be a relief to remember that, but she was too agitated to feel anything like relief.

'What about this?' He held up a pair of trousers in some fluid black fabric. 'Do they fit?'

'Yes, but you said formal. They're not—'

'At this point I'll settle for anything vaguely acceptable.' He tossed the trousers to her, already turning to the large bank of drawers.

Leila opened her mouth to protest the invasion of privacy, but he'd already opened and closed a drawer full of panties and bras and was yanking open another one. His hand plunged into silk.

Disturbingly, as he sifted through camisoles and nightwear, Leila imagined the feel of his hand on *her*, his long fingers stroking then moving on.

She staggered back a pace, horrified and a little scared at the weird sensations bombarding her. She shot out a hand to brace herself against a cupboard. Her pulse thudded too fast and there was a curious stirring in her lower body as she watched him trawl through her things.

'How about this?' He turned, a camisole of sea-green silk in his hand.

'What about it?' Her brain was slow to chug into gear.

His brows lowered. 'How about wearing it with the black pants?'

She took the proffered camisole. The silk was so fine she'd be wearing the barest whisper of covering. Did she want to dress like that when she was with Joss—a man whose gaze already evoked the strangest reactions?

She had no choice. Besides, all day she'd fretted and worried about the challenge of merely leaving the apartment. What she wore would soon pale into insignificance beside that.

'I'll try them together.' She paused, taking in his waiting stance. 'When you've left.'

With one last, impenetrable stare Joss turned and walked out. 'I'll meet you in the foyer.'

Joss stood, hands clasped behind his back, surveying the city view. But he didn't take in the glittering vista.

It was Leila he saw in his mind's eye. Spunky, sassy Leila with her air of challenge and smart mouth. Berating him in his own house! Infuriating him as no one in recent memory had been able to do.

Nearly naked Leila wearing surprisingly decorous underwear and a full-body blush that made her look like a virginal innocent, even with sexy heels and even sexier stockings accentuating the long, slender line of her legs.

He shook his head, trying to banish the vision.

How could he think her sexy when he preferred ripe, voluptuous women? True, she wasn't as bone-thin as she'd felt when he carried her on their wedding day. *Thank God for that!* According to Mrs Draycott, Leila had been eating regularly, so hopefully her extreme dieting was a thing of the past.

In fact, he'd found her slim form with its lithe curves and high, pouting breasts surprisingly arousing.

Joss wondered how Leila's pert breasts would fit in his palms. Would her hair be as soft as he imagined? Long enough perhaps to bury his face in as he gave himself up to pleasure?

He'd had no trouble calculating exactly how those long, coltish legs of hers would feel wrapped around his waist. Blood pooled heavily in his groin as he remembered her half naked and delectable, staring defiantly down her neat nose at him.

Didn't she realise he was a man who always rose to a challenge?

He stalked into the sitting room where decanters sat on a sideboard. Reaching out to pour a slug of whisky, he paused. He rarely drank. He'd watched his father, a shrewdly calculating businessman with the scruples of a barracuda, use alcohol too often to soften weaker opponents. He'd seen them lose control.

Joss was nothing if not controlled. Discipline, determination and vision had got him where he was today.

Since when had he turned to alcohol when his feelings overcame him?

Since when had he experienced *feelings*?

He jerked his hand away, heart thudding as a premonition of danger punched hard in his gut.

Yet strengthening his will didn't prevent the insidious knowledge filling his brain. That the sight of Leila, defiant and desirable, had ignited a blaze of desire within him.

He'd like to ignore his plans to network at a charity gala and instead enjoy sparring verbally with his bride.

Or exploring the fine texture of her flesh. He'd taste her sulky pouting lips and lose himself in pleasure. The sort of pleasure logic decreed should be forbidden between them.

He spun on his heel and paced, frustration soaring.

Leila was mouthy. She didn't have the richly curvaceous shape he preferred.

She had eyes that gleamed provocatively and shadowed with secrets and intrigued him as if he were some callow youth lusting after his first woman.

Joss forked his hand through his hair in exasperation. For reasons he couldn't fathom his convenient bride upset his well-ordered existence.

'I'm ready.' The husky voice swept across his senses.

Joss turned and wished he'd taken that drink.

The black trousers accentuated her feminine shape, clinging to hips and thighs. The camisole matched her eyes, making them look bigger than ever. The silk was fragile, shifting with each breath she took and shimmering invitingly over the unfettered curves of her breasts.

Heat roared in his belly as he prowled across the room to

stand before her. Her eyes widened but she didn't budge. He liked the fact she stood up to him. Or perhaps she had no notion what was on his mind.

He wanted to touch her, possess what after all was his, bought in marriage.

The appealing, insidious thought set warning lights blazing in his head.

'That's better,' he murmured, despising the effort it cost him to sound casual. 'It suits you.'

Her mouth twisted. 'It's too simple, considering you're wearing a dinner jacket. We're mismatched.'

Joss shook his head. 'Far from it. But now you mention it, the chignon doesn't suit your new look. Take it down.'

As he said it a spark of anticipation ignited.

She stared, wide-eyed for a moment, then with a half-shrug reached up to release her hair. It uncoiled in a long, glossy swinging curtain. Not straight as he'd thought but softly waving, a gentle froth of mahogany across her shoulders and halfway down her back.

Lust jabbed his vitals.

In barely there silk and nothing beneath it, with her loose hair curling around her in gentle disarray, she looked as if she'd just risen from bed.

His lower body tightened and he fought the urge to haul her to him, determined to conquer this weakness.

'Much better,' he grated through choked vocal cords. 'Let's go.'

He didn't touch her but Leila was aware of his palm hovering at the small of her back as he ushered her into the foyer.

Her pulse still raced after that scene in her dressing room. Joss's presence, his glinting stare on her half-naked body, had stolen her breath and turned her into an incoherent idiot.

Hastily she donned her coat before he could help. Call her a coward, but she preferred not to meet his eyes or feel his touch. She needed all her willpower for the hurdle to come. The moment she'd alternately feared and prepared herself for all day. When she'd face the demon of fear that had prevented her going out and exploring the city.

Too soon the plush, mirrored lift arrived.

Leila took a step towards it and halted, heels squeaking in protest on the marble floor.

'Leila?' He stood aside so she could precede him.

She took another staccato step, only to stop on the threshold, her heart hammering out of control.

Was it the thought of leaving the apartment or the sight of that confined space that sent anxious fingers clawing at her lungs?

Leila had spent too long locked in a space not much bigger than that. Even today after weeks of trying she'd not managed to stay in the lift long enough to reach the foyer.

An off-key laugh escaped her lips.

She'd prided herself on the fact Gamil hadn't broken her will and she'd remained strong. Now had she developed a fear of wide-open spaces and small ones too?

It was preposterous. Absurd. Terrifying.

Fury as well as fear surged in her veins. At Gamil for bringing her to this. At herself for succumbing.

At Joss for being here to witness it.

'Have you forgotten something?'

Leila cast a quick glance upwards, seeing that firm chin and that lavishly sculpted lower lip. She swallowed an obstruction in her throat. Maybe if she concentrated on Joss…

'Leila?' His tone was impatient.

On a rush of determination she stepped over the threshold, her body chilling instantly as if she'd walked into a deep freeze.

She felt Joss enter behind her, his big hand at her waist. If she focused on the feel of his palm, maybe she could push aside the terror eating at her.

The sinister hiss of the doors closing almost stopped her breath. She swung round, her hand already raised to slam the control that would open the door.

Her hand hit a deep chest, a smooth lapel. Hard fingers wrapped around hers, pressing her palm to the rhythmic thud of Joss's heart.

'What is it, Leila?'

She shook her head, barely conscious of the unfamiliar caress of unbound hair on naked shoulders and arms. She pressed forward, swallowing convulsively, trying to move him, to reach the controls before the panic gnawing at her stomach got the better of her.

He didn't budge, just stood blocking her escape.

'I've changed my mind.' Her voice was raw. 'I don't want to go out.' Desperation drove her. This cramped lift was bad enough, but then she faced the vast space that was the city of London—huge and sprawling and as terrifying as the desert had been. Leila tried a shaky sidestep but Joss's hand clamped hers. His grasp tightened at her waist.

'It's too late for that!'

'I don't care…' The words clogged in her throat as her chest constricted.

A large hand tilted her chin. Blazing midnight-dark eyes held hers. She shoved at his chest, needing to make him open the door, even as the lift descended with a sudden slide that rearranged all her internal organs.

'Let me out!' Terror made the words a glacial command.

Hazily she saw his perplexed scowl and the flash of ire. One solid arm wrapped round her back and hard fingers angled her jaw up, his thumb hot on her frozen cheek.

'You really are some piece of work,' he mused. 'Is this a game to make me jump to your tune because I made you change? Your stepfather may have allowed you to play the spoiled princess but you're with me now, sweetheart.'

For the length of one heartbeat he stared. Then his lips

tilted into a grim smile. 'I won't be made a fool of, Leila. We play by my rules now.'

Then his head swooped down, blocking the light.

CHAPTER SIX

JOSS'S MOUTH SLAMMED into hers with a precision that spoke of furious control and deadly expertise. His arm at her waist lashed tight, securing her against his unforgiving frame. His hand on her face held her uncompromisingly still.

Not that there was anywhere to escape. Nowhere except the tiny, enclosed lift.

A tiny sob welled in her throat. A sob of frustration and despair that for all her vaunted strength she had no weapons to fight this new challenge. Not when the fear came from within.

How could she fight the weakness when it was inside her head?

Joss's mouth moved expertly on hers, shaping its contours, his head tilting overhead.

Heat, darkness, danger. She didn't know if she tasted them on his lips or absorbed them with the air she tried frantically to drag into her lungs.

The spice scent that had intrigued earlier filled her nostrils and she knew it for *his* scent. Not bottled, but the fragrance of his skin, unique and intrinsically masculine.

His mouth moved again and now it was different. His tongue thrust into her mouth: conquering, demanding and giving no quarter.

Leila shuddered as a riptide of unfamiliar sensations flooded her. There was no allowance for inexperience. No concession for the thrill of fear skimming her spine, only a demanding caress that felt like invasion.

Except that a tiny part of her responded to his uncompromising demand.

A tingle shot to her breasts, shivered lower still, at the sensations evoked by Joss's sweeping tongue. His mouth pressed like a challenge against her lips. Her eyes flickered closed on welcoming darkness.

His fingers splayed over her cheek, slipping into her hair.

Then somehow, without deciding to, Leila was kissing him back, ravenously, clumsily, as the dregs of fear morphed into angry hunger.

She wanted so much to *live. Experience. To be free.*

For years she'd been thwarted by her stepfather and now, on the brink of freedom, by fear and a husband who wouldn't let her be.

Gloriously, furiously angry, Leila clutched the satin lapels of Joss's dinner jacket. She stretched up, bringing the kiss to him, delving daringly into his hot velvet mouth. Pressing against him with a surging need for something: sensation, validation, pleasure, she didn't know which.

He tasted mysterious. Perilously addictive.

Part of her stunned brain, the minuscule part still working, catalogued that *this* was how a man tasted. How he felt. Joss's iron-hard frame against hers was more exciting than anything she'd known. Except the way their tongues thrust and tangled. Rivulets of molten sensation poured into her bloodstream. Sparking shards of fire cascaded through her.

She wanted more.

More of the luscious heat. The heady thrill of unleashed emotion in such delicious counterpoint to that leashed masculine power.

For, despite the ravaging intensity of the kiss, she sensed Joss restrained himself. He was rock solid, unmoving, except for his mouth and the hand caressing her scalp in se-

ductively slow circles, drawing the fear and anger away. Yet
it did nothing to lessen the tension building inside. A different sort of tension.

Pleasure ignited. It burned brighter than the fear that had
crowded her or the fury born of frustration that had catapulted her into responding.

Her hands slid up Joss's chest, past the quick thud of his
heart. Her fingers grazed the hot skin of his neck, his jaw,
before tunnelling into thick locks of silk.

Leila heard a low growl. A growl of need and satisfaction, and had no idea if it came from her or him. She simply
wanted more of this magic.

With her arms over his shoulders her body stretched
against his. Hot shivers of delight racked her. Her breasts
grazed silk and the heavy friction of Joss's chest, drawing
her nipples into hard little nubs.

Could he feel them?

The thought excited her unbearably.

The arm around her slid up and a large palm curved round
her, burrowing beneath her coat. She'd swear it branded her
through the gossamer silk of her top. Long fingers swirled
lazily at her side, skimmed higher, brushing the side of her
breast in a teasing, deliberate move that sent a jolt of response
through her.

Leila sagged, clutching Joss's thick hair, waiting for his
next touch.

This time it was heavier, moulding to the side of her breast
before sliding down to her waist.

She moaned, holding Joss's head in a fierce embrace as
she poured out her need into a kiss that grew slow and lush
despite the urgency escalating inside her. A pulse throbbed
low between her legs.

His hand circled her waist then slid down her bottom, fingers splayed. With a jerk he tugged her close and high till
she was pressed to the length of him. Solid thighs supported

hers. She moulded to that broad chest and hard belly, and to the long, hot ridge of arousal that even a woman as inexperienced as Leila couldn't mistake.

She gasped at his blatant need. Fire poured through her, pooling low as she gave in to temptation and rubbed against him. He felt glorious.

Their kiss grew sumptuous, heavy with promise.

Ribbons of heat unravelled through her, weighting her limbs. Leila pressed closer.

Joss's hands clamped hard on her buttocks, drawing her higher so their bodies aligned perfectly.

Bliss beckoned.

Something vibrated against her chest. A low buzz of sound penetrated the syrupy haze of bliss.

There was stillness but for the beat of hearts pounding in unison and the heated pulse of Joss's breath in her mouth—and that low buzzing.

Then his hands were on her upper arms as his mouth lifted. She gasped for air, her breath raw and loud.

Did he realise she was in danger of slumping boneless at his feet? Was that why he held her so hard?

Dazed, she catalogued his rumpled hair and the smear of lipstick at the corner of his mouth.

She wanted to lean back in and taste his mouth again. Till she lifted her gaze and saw the glint in his eyes.

At last Leila found the presence of mind to stumble back, away from that knowing scrutiny. She grasped the rail on the lift wall to keep herself upright since her legs had dissolved into quivering jelly.

She blinked, taking in the fact the lift had stopped moving. They'd reached the basement without her realising!

Joss reached for his phone and Leila could only stare. She hadn't even connected the buzzing vibrations with anything as prosaic as a mobile phone. She'd been on another plane entirely.

A strange hollow ache engulfed her, as if Joss had scooped out her insides.

Her lips throbbed, tingling in the aftermath of that punishing kiss. No, not punishing, not after that first moment. Thrilling. Exciting. Soul-destroying.

Her fingers tightened on the rail as he turned away and spoke into the phone. Leila concentrated on deep breaths, trying to slow her galloping pulse. And all the while she felt as if she'd stepped off a precipice into a world she didn't recognise.

It was only as silence filled her ears that she realised she'd shut her eyes, trying to gather the tattered remnants of control.

Gathering her strength Leila opened her eyes. A crisp white shirt faced her. A tuxedo, unbuttoned. She lifted her gaze to a bow tie half undone and rakishly trailing.

She forced herself to look up past that firm chin, past compressed lips that mere moments ago had taken her by storm, to glittering midnight-blue eyes that seared straight into her soul.

Tension screamed through her as she fought for strength to deal with him. Leila's brows knitted as her brain supplied the words she'd been avoiding.

Her husband.

He was her husband and he'd kissed her as if there were no tomorrow! As if nothing mattered but the combustible desire that had engulfed them.

Where had that come from?

And more importantly, would he now expect—

'After you.'

Leila frowned, then saw he held the door open.

Automatically she stepped forward, careful not to brush against him lest that shocking heat, that need, swamp her again.

It was only much later that she realised she'd faced the cavernous underground car park then the open streets of London without a tremor of the fear that had haunted her since the wedding.

She'd been so wrapped in shock over her response to Joss Carmody's sizzling kiss, so aware of his even breathing, his tall frame so near, his seductive power, there'd been no room for anything else.

Leila stood out from the throng like a diamond of the first water among overbright imitations.

Joss had sensed it from the first—her innate class. Not class in the way his snobbish mother, granddaughter of an earl and weighed down by her expectation of privilege, had used the word. But class in the sense of unmistakeable quality.

Even underdressed by the standards around her, Leila shone. Joss had to force his gaze from the tempting high thrust of her breasts, naked beneath thin silk.

Knowing precisely how underdressed she was made the evening a trial. He had no time to be bored with the social flim-flam because most of his brain was engaged in remembering how she'd felt in his arms.

And imagining how she'd feel naked beneath him as he thrust between her lissom thighs.

Heat poured across his skin as it tightened in arousal.

This wasn't supposed to happen, not with *her*.

Joss wasn't interested in a relationship with any woman that lasted more than a night. He wouldn't destroy his peace, and his plans to use Leila to further his commercial interests, by having sex. She'd want more—of his time or attention or, God help him, his emotions. It had happened before. Women always wanted more of him, not understanding he had nothing more to give.

And they hadn't been married to him! How much higher Leila's expectations if he succumbed to the lure of carnal satisfaction that brewed potent and dark in his veins?

He gave a huff of self-disgust and tried to tune in to Leila charming Boris Tevchenko, key investor in a major consortium with interests in Bakhara.

Instead Joss's focus lingered on her lips, now turned up from their natural sultry pout into a smile.

Joss recognised it as the polite smile she wore as easily as make-up, part of her repertoire of charm. Not as breathtaking as the no-holds-barred grin she'd given him when he'd taken her onto his plane, but enough to bedazzle most men.

Boris looked dazzled.

Joss wondered at his surge of discontent. Leila had the Russian eating out of her palm. Wasn't that what he wanted?

Yet Joss felt edgy, aware of the buzz of interest Leila had stirred, not liking the hungry glances sent her way.

He'd never felt possessive of a woman.

He'd never been married before. That had to be it.

Joss slid his arm through Leila's, drawing her to him. Her start of surprise was natural since she hadn't seen him move closer. But the stiff way she held herself, as if repelling more intimacies, sent anger surging through him.

He was her husband and she'd have to get used to his touch in public.

'So, Boris, you're interested in my plans for the Bakhari plain?'

The other man shrugged, his eyes flicking back to Leila. 'Possibly. Though right now your lovely wife interests me more.'

Her laugh was light and musical. It was only the second time Joss had heard it, and it arrested him. Like some moonstruck kid! 'Boris, I appreciate the compliment—' she leaned in conspiratorially '—but you're an astute businessman. How could you not be interested in the last, vast untapped oil reserves in the Middle East?'

'How, indeed?' A harsh baritone made Joss turn to meet the shrewd eyes of Asad Murat as he joined them.

Excellent. London-based Murat was one of the men he'd come to meet and one of the reasons Leila would be valuable, because of her family connections with Murat. No doubt that was why Murat had approached after proving elusive earlier.

Everything was coming together nicely. Attending this function had been worth it after all.

'Tevchenko. Carmody.' The newcomer nodded to the men before flashing a glance at Leila, but to Joss's surprise offered her no greeting.

Beside him Leila stood rigid. Annoyance stirred as Joss felt tension hum through her. Clearly she disdained his touch.

How could she object to his hand on her arm after she'd wrapped herself around him an hour ago? She'd been all over him. They'd have had sex up against the lift wall if it hadn't been for that phone call.

Heat spiked and his groin tightened uncomfortably. He hadn't been thinking with his head when he'd kissed Leila.

Hadn't he known a wife would bring complications?

Murat turned to Joss. 'Aren't you concerned about over-extending yourself with this new venture? You've had oil-rig trouble and didn't I hear about unrest in that African gold mine? Labour problems?'

Leila lifted her glass of sparkling mineral water to parched lips. Casually she glanced around the room as if her heart hadn't dived at the sight of her stepfather Gamil's crony.

She had herself in hand now. When Asad Murat had looked at her as if she were some insect he planned to skewer with a pin, she'd wanted to dash her drink in his face.

She was proud she'd kept her poise. No matter that Murat had approved and encouraged Gamil's maltreatment of her. He'd been a regular visitor to the house and she'd seen enough to know he and Gamil were two of a kind.

He hated being ignored by her. Even now he darted curious glances her way while in discussion with Joss.

Leila had no intention of talking to her husband about the past. She wanted to believe Joss wasn't like Gamil. He was bossy and accustomed to getting what he wanted, but she hadn't seen a sadistic streak.

Yet she wouldn't put it to the test. Revealing how she'd been dominated in the past was revealing a weakness.

Her husband was dangerous enough. Look at the way he'd kissed her in the lift. The way he'd made her *feel*. She couldn't believe she'd unravelled in his arms. She didn't even *like* him.

A tremor rippled through her, arrowing between her thighs, as she remembered their bodies locked together.

As if he was responding to her thoughts, Joss's grip tightened and he drew her close.

Her traitorous body wanted to melt against him. Only the memory of that kiss stopped her. And the sight of Asad Murat watching through narrowed eyes.

Revulsion filled her. If this was the sort of man Joss associated with, she needed to be on her guard.

'I'll fetch Mrs Carmody to the phone, sir.'

'She's at home, then?'

'Oh, yes, sir.' His housekeeper paused. 'She's always home.'

Joss opened his mouth to query further, then realised it was no business of his what Leila did with her time. He wasn't interested. So long as she was discreet and fulfilled the function he required as his hostess.

Though the idea of Leila being *discreet* with another man gnawed at him. Maybe because the men at last night's reception had all but salivated over her.

He yanked at his tie as he waited for his wife to pick up. *His wife.*

Damn it. He'd spent last night trying not to think about her as his wife. That according to custom she should have spent the night in his bed, finishing what they'd begun with that kiss. That he wanted her more than he could remember wanting any woman.

After one taste!

'Joss?' Her voice was husky, making heat spool low in his groin.

He cleared his throat. 'Leila. I'm glad I caught you.'

'Yes?' Her tone was wary. Why? What had she been up to? Ruthlessly Joss crushed a surge of jealous curiosity.

'I have plans for tonight and thought I'd better warn you.' He paused but she said nothing.

What did he expect? That she'd gush and chatter? She'd been silent on the trip home last night, withdrawn in her corner of the limo and distant even as they made their way up to the penthouse. If he hadn't been busy calculating some new business connections, he'd have been annoyed at her abstraction. She hadn't even looked at him—had been lost in reverie.

'We're going to dinner tonight with some associates and then, if things go well, I'll continue the discussions in the penthouse over port and coffee. I thought you'd need notice to prepare.'

'To look the part of a tycoon's wife, you mean?' Was that a huff of amusement?

'Well, you can't wear anything currently in your wardrobe. I want you looking chic and sophisticated.' He paused but again she said nothing. He wished he could see her face and know what she was thinking. Then he caught the direction of his thoughts and annoyance stirred. 'You know how, I presume?'

'I told you, I didn't choose those clothes.' Was that anger in her voice? Why did her reaction, *any* reaction, feel like a victory?

'Yet you did nothing to replace them.'

'Because I didn't have the money.'

'What?'

'You heard me, Joss. I've been waiting for the first of the payments you're supposed to provide.'

He frowned. 'I've been away, you know that. Tied up.'

What did a week or so matter? He'd had more urgent matters on his mind than her allowance. 'Couldn't you have used your own money in the interim?' Was she trying to make him feel *guilty*?

'According to the prenuptial agreement that money *is* mine. I earned it when I married you, remember?'

He stiffened. She made it sound as if he were some undesirable who had to pay a woman to marry him! He recalled the number of women who'd angled for permanency in his life. It was ironic that the bride he'd tied himself to viewed him as a necessary burden.

'What are you laughing at?' Her voice was suspicious.

'Nothing. But I don't understand why you haven't been shopping. You've got all London at your disposal.'

'I told you.' This time her voice was low, as if the words were drawn out unwillingly. 'I don't have any money.'

'That's impossible!' Joss paused, waiting for her to contradict him. She said nothing. 'Leila? How is that possible?'

'I inherited land, not money. And you now have the land, remember?' Her clipped tone warned him off further questions.

Joss ignored it. 'What about the money you already had? Surely there was plenty to cover a new wardrobe?' She was an heiress. Her stepfather was wealthy in his own right and her family was one of Bakhara's oldest. 'Leila?'

'Do you really think I'd have dressed as I did last night if I'd had a choice?' His nape prickled as he heard bitterness lace her words.

She wasn't joking. Hell! How could it be?

His image of her, all his certainties, fractured.

He opened his mouth to demand an explanation, but stopped himself.

Did he want to embroil himself in the details of Leila's past? He'd spent too many hours already pondering his beautiful, enigmatic bride. She'd distracted him as he'd sought to network and his concentration this morning had been shot. *Because of her.*

'You should have told me.'

'You weren't here to tell.' She paused. 'I could have phoned your office and left a message but frankly the idea of explaining to a third party—'

'I'll have the arrangements made immediately.' Joss swiped a hand over his jaw, as if he could rub away the shard of guilt that pierced him. He supposed he should have given her his mobile number before he left. The fact that he was unused to being tied to anyone was no excuse.

'Someone will contact you within the hour with details of your new account and how to access it.'

He wouldn't give her cause to claim he'd reneged on their marriage bargain. Too much rode on it.

And as for his wife?

He set his jaw. He couldn't avoid it any longer. It was time he satisfied his curiosity about her.

CHAPTER SEVEN

LEILA PACED the sitting room, schooling herself not to twitch the slippery fabric of her new dress that clung and caressed in the most unfamiliar, sensual way.

Sophisticated, Joss had ordered in that offhand tone. *Chic.* And then he'd had the gall to ask her if she could manage that! His tone had reminded her again of her place in his world: mere window dressing for his schemes.

Pride smarting, Leila had aimed instead for *spectacular*.

She refused to be dismissed and ordered about by another arrogant man. She'd show Joss she was a thinking, feeling, capable woman who demanded respect!

She bit her lip and spun on one spindly heel, her heart diving. She felt like a sham.

How to convince him she was worthy of respect when she hadn't got the nerve to leave this apartment? The only time she'd left was last night, with him. When the emotions he aroused had eclipsed all else.

Today she'd tried again alone and been overwhelmed by wrenching nausea at the prospect of stepping outside.

Leila's nails dug into her palms, hating that even now Gamil had a hold over her. She had no doubt her imprisonment at his hands, and the stress of living with his unpredictable moods, had led to this…weakness.

Even this gorgeous new dress was courtesy of a personal

shopper who'd arrived at the penthouse, bringing a bewildering array of outfits for approval.

Joss had been as good as his word. She'd had money of her own within thirty minutes of their phone call. The first money of her own in years! That fact sent a tingle of excitement down her backbone. Money meant a level of independence that had been too long denied her.

No wonder she'd splurged on some extras as well as the clothing she needed. Leila surveyed the colourful scatter cushions enlivening the austere furniture and the bowls of fresh flowers, all ordered by phone or online.

And there was money enough to begin saving a nest egg. One day she'd find a way out of the legal agreement that kept her here at her husband's pleasure. Then she'd be truly free.

'Leila, you're ready.' The words cut across her thoughts and made her stiffen.

Joss stood just inside the doorway, handsome in a craggy, rough-around-the-edges way that oozed raw masculinity. Her breath snagged. He looked more vital, more potently alive than any man she'd ever seen.

Reluctantly Leila met his eyes. A sizzle of raw power arced across the room and sparks fizzed through her.

Her gaze dropped helplessly to his firm, sculpted mouth. She swallowed hard, remembering the taste of him on her lips, the feel of being swept hard into his embrace, of going up in flames against his body.

'Hello, Joss. How are you?' Her voice dropped to a throaty murmur when she'd intended to sound unaffected.

For a moment he seemed not to register her words. His stare had a fixed quality. Then he paced into the room. 'Well, thank you. And you?'

'Fine.' Her smile was perfunctory. She'd told herself the stress of last night had skewed her perceptions. That she'd imagined him more compelling and disturbing than he really was.

She'd been wrong. One look and her body came alive in ways she hadn't known till that kiss… No, she couldn't afford to think about that.

The glint in his eyes drew her skin tight. For a man who saw her as merely a social asset his gaze was incredibly intense.

'Sophisticated enough for you?' she asked finally, gesturing to the gown of sea-green silk shot with misty grey she'd loved at first sight.

Still no reply.

Her assurance cracked. Had she fooled herself into thinking this worked?

Gamil had removed the mirrors from the house years ago. Maybe she'd lost her discernment in that time?

Annoyed for letting doubt in, Leila reminded herself she didn't care what Joss thought. She liked the dress and that was what mattered. It made her feel good.

Setting her chin, she lifted her arms a fraction and turned on the spot with exaggerated slowness. Her mother's pearl pendant, with its platinum chain fully extended, swung gently against her bare back where the deep V of the dress, mirroring a shallower V at the front, revealed a daring amount of flesh.

She'd decided to wear the pendant that way in a flash of bravado, annoyed at Joss's brusque demand over the phone. She'd wanted to look eye-catching.

Now, with his gaze fixed on her, she wasn't so sure.

A ripple of sensation tensed her muscles as he closed in on her. Automatically her jaw angled higher lest he guess the strange jittering unsteadiness inside her.

'Perfect,' he murmured. 'You look gorgeous.'

Really? She was stunned at her surge of delight.

Her father had called her pretty but since his death no man had complimented her on her looks. Not that many had been given the chance!

Now she read appreciation in Joss's eyes. After years of

being berated and denigrated, a compliment was a shock. It did wonders for her bruised ego. But it also, like tenderness after years of abuse, threatened her composure.

Dismayed, she blinked and lowered her gaze a little, battling a sudden tightness in her chest.

'Thank you,' she said when she found her voice. 'You do too.'

Joss's mouth lifted on one side, driving a crease down his cheek. It emphasised the sexy curve of his mouth and the wholly masculine set of his chin.

Jerkily she reached for her purse. 'Shall we go?'

'After you.' He gestured for her to precede him.

'I hear you've had a visitor,' he said a moment later.

She shrugged, hypersensitive to the barely-there silk swishing around her with each step and the weight of the pearl heavy between her naked shoulder blades.

'I engaged a personal shopper.'

'Ah.' Joss drew out the monosyllable. 'And I gather there was a man too, several days ago.'

Leila slammed to a halt, glacial ice crackling down her spine. Even facing the daily frustration of her new-found fear of going out, Leila had believed herself free. She thought she'd left spies and coercion behind.

She swung round, meeting Joss's dark eyes with a blaze of fury. 'Is your staff spying on me?'

'Of course not.'

Her fingers bit the beaded softness of her bag. 'Then how do you know about my visitors?'

For what seemed an age Joss stood, watching her, his scrutiny sharp enough to take in her blush of rage and the pulse thundering in her throat.

'Mrs Draycott was worried.' He spoke slowly, almost gently. 'She said you seemed upset after he'd gone.'

With a hiss of air escaping from tight lungs, Leila's ire dissipated, leaving her off balance. She wasn't used to anyone worrying about her, had forgotten what it felt like.

'Leila? Who was he?' Amazingly she registered concern in Joss's voice. It stroked her like the brush of finest velvet, far more potent even than his admiration.

She was tempted to say it was none of his business who her visitor had been. But what was the point? 'A lawyer I consulted about the marriage contract. And as for being upset...' she shrugged '...I was just preoccupied.'

Worry about how she'd pay for that legal advice had been just an extra burden to add to the rest. She'd had no difficulty getting a private consultation—lawyers were used to visiting rich clients. But at the time Leila thought she'd have to sell her mother's jewellery to pay for the privilege if she didn't soon get the money to which she was entitled.

'I see.' Yet still Joss's frown lingered, as if he wanted to know more.

What was there to know? The contract was watertight. She abided by it or returned to Bakhara and Gamil's tender mercies. Stoically she repressed a shudder. She'd do anything rather than face that.

She turned and walked down the hall.

'Mrs Draycott also said you haven't left the apartment.'

Leila stiffened, but kept walking. 'Did she?'

'Yes.' He was so close she could swear she felt his warm breath on the back of her neck. Rills of sensation rayed out from the spot.

'I had a busy few weeks preparing for the wedding. I needed a rest.'

'You'll make yourself ill if you don't get some fresh air and exercise.'

Leila kept walking. 'Still afraid I'm anorexic?' She gritted her teeth. That accusation still rankled. 'Or did you hear my appetite's improved lately?'

Silence.

She'd been right! He *had* been checking on her. No doubt he wanted to make sure his shiny new trophy wife was fit for duty.

Impotent fury spurred her on as she entered the foyer, her heels clicking furiously on gleaming marble.

So much for being free! She was Joss's captive, though her cage was lavishly sumptuous.

The knowledge beat a heavy tattoo in her heart. She *would* find a way out of this.

'If you must know,' she said when the silence between them drew tight, 'I've been using the indoor pool to exercise.'

After her close confinement those laps had almost killed her to start with but she'd refused to give in. With her returning appetite and decent sleep, she was starting to build her strength. She felt better for it.

'I apologise.' His voice was gruff. 'I was…concerned.' Leila paused, caught by the note of something she couldn't read in his voice. Something that eased the fiery anger inside.

Beside her a long arm reached out and pressed the button for the lift. Immediately butterflies the size of kites dipped and whirled in her stomach. Her mouth dried.

The door swished open with a hiss like a venomous snake.

Leila stared at the mirrored wall at the back of the lift and stepped in before she could have second thoughts. She tried to focus on the reflection of her chic gown and Joss, tall and broodingly handsome behind her. But it was the small airless space that consumed her attention. And the fact that straight after this she'd face the wide-open streets of the city.

With each breath her pulse quickened.

'Leila?' Joss held the door open with one hand and she wanted to scream at him to shut the doors and get this over quickly.

'Yes?' Her voice echoed hollowly.

'Are you okay?'

'Just brilliant.' Her smile was a rictus grin but she couldn't prevent it. Her nails clawed the delicate purse.

'You don't look it.' Those penetrating eyes were fixed on her face as if they read every thought.

Tremors raced down Leila's spine, drawing her skin so she felt stretched on a rack of tension that screwed tighter with each slow motion moment. Her muscles ached with the force of fighting the impulse to flee straight back into the safety of the apartment.

It took everything she had to fight her fear.

Still he didn't move, just stood there, prolonging the agony.

With a suddenness that surprised him Leila lunged, grabbed him by the arm and hauled him inside. Her other hand slammed onto the control panel, sending the doors swishing shut.

This close he saw dampness bloom on her forehead and upper lip. She was pale, her features drawn.

Another punch of the controls set the lift plunging.

Leila's hand tightened like a talon on his arm and she stared fixedly at his shirt as if memorising every detail.

'Leila?' Her absolute concentration unnerved him. What was he missing?

'Yes?'

'Look at me.' She didn't move.

'Leila!' At his sharp tone her head swung up. His heart kicked hard against his ribs as shock smacked him. Her pupils had dilated so far her eyes looked black, only a tiny circle of crystalline green glittering at the edges.

Joss covered her hand with his, feeling her tremble.

She was afraid!

It was remarkable, inexplicable, but true.

He raised his hands to her cheeks. They were clammy. He tried to convince himself there was another explanation but none made sense.

His brain clicked in rapid replay.

Had it been fear earlier in the lift? When he'd taken her sudden change of mind for a spoiled woman's wilful games?

Fear too that day she'd half collapsed on the way to the plane?

And what about last night returning to the apartment when she'd sat statue-still in the far corner of the limo's wide back seat? He'd thought her lost in private reverie.

What if, instead, Leila had been frozen with fear?

Suddenly, appallingly, Mrs Draycott's comment about Leila not leaving the premises made awful sense. And the fact that instead of going out to meet friends or shop, she'd had visitors come to her.

Joss wanted to reject the mind-blowing suspicion, but couldn't. It fitted together too neatly.

Why hadn't he put it together before?

Because he'd had more important things on his mind than his bride.

A searing blade of guilt skewered him.

He, of all people, knew what happened to the weak when no one took time to notice and respond to their fears. Hadn't he told himself Joanna would still be alive if someone had taken a real interest in his sister?

Yet Leila wasn't weak. Even collapsing in his arms at the airport she'd been adamant about continuing the journey. The woman who'd just berated him for nosing about her private business was no weakling.

He looked into those unfocused eyes, remembering how she'd yanked him into the lift and slammed the button for the underground car park. She might be scared but she wasn't running. She faced fear head-on, with a reckless disregard for her well-being.

Joss's gut tightened at her valiant, confronting courage.

'Speak to me, Leila.'

'What do you want me to say?' She spoke slowly, the words thick on her tongue, as if she had trouble talking.

He couldn't believe this was the woman who moments before had tossed barbed comments at him.

'Tell me what you're scared of.' He had a pretty good idea, but he needed to hear it from her.

'I'm not scared of anything.' Yet her words were slurred, her eyes unfocused. Beneath his hands she shivered. Did he imagine her growing colder by the moment?

It was a lifetime since he'd worried about anyone, except in the impersonal way an employer took responsibility for his workers' safety. This didn't feel impersonal. It felt frighteningly *real*.

Joss's hold firmed as he recalled their kiss last time they descended his private lift. At least then she hadn't been frozen with terror. She'd been all vibrant, hot passion.

'Kiss me, Leila.' His voice was husky as he bent to meet her lips.

She jerked back, swaying till he caught her in a gentle grip. This was for her own good, he assured himself.

'No.' But her voice had lost its strength. Where were her sassy comebacks? That, more than anything, convinced him this was real, not a product of his imagination.

Joss threaded his fingers through her perfectly coiffed hair, tugging it loose. The fact she didn't stop him added to his alarm. He massaged her scalp and brushed his lips across hers as she stood perfectly still. Back again, feeling the soft swell of her bottom lip, the infinitesimal caress of warm air in his mouth as a sigh escaped her parted lips.

A thread of sensation unravelled in his belly as if in response to the most erotic lover's touch. The power of it took him by surprise.

And still she didn't move.

His lips firmed, slanting to cover hers as his tongue slid along those sultry lips. He reminded himself this wasn't about sex. It was about…what? Saving her from fear? That wasn't the whole truth.

His interest was personal.

Her mouth moved against his and a jolt of sensation speared him. Relief or pleasure?

Joss didn't analyse. He drew her closer, one arm wrapped around her, his palm pressed to her bare spine, capturing the pearl that had swayed so tantalisingly against her flawless skin as she sashayed in front of him to the lift.

Her skin was cool but it warmed to his touch as her mouth moved carefully under his, mirroring each gentle caress.

The sensation of her lips accommodating his, opening with a sigh at the lunge of his exploring tongue, was deliciously provocative. She tasted like desire and honeyed promise. Like the most luscious exotic fruit.

Dimly he heard the lift ping and the slide of the doors. Instead of moving, Joss gathered her in, wanting to prolong the almost innocent pleasure of her tentative response.

There was nothing innocent about the surge of possessive hunger that urged him to haul her back to the penthouse and into bed. Fire shot to Joss's groin and his embrace hardened. Her bare back was silken beneath his palm. Her mouth sweet distraction.

Even the touch of her palms, pressed flat to his jacket, heightened his carnal senses. He wanted those gentle fingers on his bare body, all over him.

Would she mark him with her nails in the throes of ecstasy? He'd wager she was as passionate in bed as she was when she fought him. Joss's skin tightened in a shiver of pure lust as he imagined Leila naked beneath him. Those pert breasts thrusting up into his palms, her throaty moans husky in his ears as he drove them both to a pinnacle of bliss.

Joss's hold tightened convulsively and suddenly Leila wasn't kissing him back.

With a wrench she broke free.

Disbelieving, Joss watched the rapid rise and fall of her breasts with dazed fascination.

'Don't look at me like that!'

He jerked his head up.

Huge eyes of cloudy emerald held his beneath heavy lids, as if she too had difficulty shaking off the erotic force of that kiss. Her hair was a mass of rich, dark waves around her shoulders, framing a face now flushed instead of pale. Her mouth was bare of lipstick and her lips looked plump and poutingly kissable.

Joss shoved his hands into his pockets before he could reach for her again.

'I'm not on tap for your pleasure.' Her eyes narrowed to slits of sizzling fire. Challenge vibrated in every taut line of her body.

Someone should warn her that he thrived on challenge. He had only one way of dealing with it: facing it head-on and winning. Every time.

It was all Joss could do not to haul her up against him and demonstrate how flimsy her outrage was. She'd kissed him back; there'd been no mistaking her shudder of pleasure as she'd leaned in.

'Did you hear me?'

'I heard you, Leila.' Even saying her name, after tasting her breath in his mouth, was a sensual experience. His eyes dropped to the jerky pulse at the base of her neck. Would her skin taste as delicious as her lips?

Suddenly he was ravenous with the need to find out.

He didn't need Leila's outraged expression to warn him he was on dangerous ground. He knew already. He'd been in treacherous territory all week as he spent hours pondering his intriguing wife instead of concentrating on work.

But even that didn't deter him.

Success was all about making plans then adapting them to suit emerging needs.

His lips twisted in a mirthless grin. What he felt for Leila was definitely an emerging need.

Was it possible he'd miscalculated, demanding this be a paper marriage only?

Would it be so very bad if he mixed a little personal pleasure with business after all?

'You can stop looking at me as if you'd like to...'

'Eat you all up?' Joss couldn't prevent his wolfish grin as anticipation weighted his lower body.

Leila's eyes widened, her mouth sagging a fraction before she snapped it shut.

Was that genuine shock? The idea intrigued Joss, and excited him. He was tired, he discovered suddenly, of women so experienced they were blasé about life and everything in it except money.

Leila would never be boring or predictable.

Even now she was primming her lips as if she'd like to punish him.

He'd enjoy watching her try.

'Don't put your hair up.' Already she was twisting it high at the back of her head in quick movements. He enjoyed seeing her long tresses around her shoulders. Last night he'd found one excuse after another to draw her close just to feel its softness and inhale its fragrance.

Leila shook her head curtly. 'Not with this dress.'

As she spoke she turned away, presenting him with a view of her sleek back, the graceful curve of her spine ridiculously alluring. The dress was completely decent, covering breasts, arms and most of her legs, yet something about that deep V of bare feminine flesh made his body prickle with renewed hunger.

His.

Leila was his.

The covetous thought filled his brain to the exclusion of all else.

Until he saw her stiffen as she faced the open door to the

vast underground car park. Her shoulders hunched and he heard her suck in her breath.

Belatedly his brain notched into gear and he remembered her anxiety. The fact that she didn't venture out, except last night when he'd given her no option.

He wanted to know more, to understand. But now wasn't the time.

Joss stepped close and slid his arm under hers, wrapped her hand over his and clamped it there, noting the way she held onto him as if fearing he'd let her go. It stirred a long-dormant protectiveness.

'This way.' He nodded towards the waiting limo he used in London. He preferred his driving off road and fast, not at a snail's pace in city streets.

He made to step forward but Leila stood her ground. She refused to go with him? Was she that scared?

He looked down and saw the determined angle of Leila's chin.

'I can walk alone.' She relaxed her grip, inviting him to release her. 'There's no need to act the doting husband.' Her tone was light and high as if her breathing was too shallow, but Joss couldn't mistake the fierce glitter of pride in her eyes.

So much for admitting she was anxious. She was toughing it out, pretending a calmness belied by the tiny tremors he felt racing through her body.

Something stirred deep inside him.

He liked that she was a fighter, refusing to give in. He could relate to that. Obstinacy was the quality that had helped him survive life with his self-absorbed parents and move on.

'Just getting in a little practice for our dinner guests.' He shrugged. 'I'm not used to being part of a couple. I need to get it right.'

Which was a lie. Few things had felt so instantly right as holding Leila.

'Very well.' She drew in a deep breath and Joss battled

to keep his gaze on her face. 'You can take my arm.' She sounded like a gracious monarch bestowing a concession. 'But let's get this clear. I don't appreciate being manhandled.'

Her gaze skimmed his face to rest at a point near his collar.

Not so brave after all. Was she afraid of what she might see in his face, or of herself? There'd been two of them kissing a moment ago.

'If you want kisses—' her voice was low '—find someone else to share them.'

'You're not interested?' he persisted, daring her to lie outright.

'Why should I be?' Leila lifted her eyes to his. He felt for an absurd moment as if he were drowning in a pure pool of deep mountain water. 'I kissed you yesterday out of curiosity.' She lifted her shoulders in a tight shrug. 'That doesn't mean I want to repeat it.'

'No?' She could have fooled him. Yesterday it had been more than curiosity driving her. But he'd cut her some slack. He'd seen her fear mere minutes ago. It hit him that he never wanted to see her like that again.

'No.' Gripping his hand firmly, Leila stepped out into the vast subterranean space, her attention locked on the car waiting for them. 'After all, it wasn't in our contract, was it?'

CHAPTER EIGHT

'I'D ALWAYS HEARD you were lucky as well as clever. Now I know it's true.'

Joss looked at the Russian beside him and raised his eyebrows. 'Really?' Tevchenko was one of Europe's wealthiest men. Joss's London apartment, though expensive and perfectly positioned, Joss had chosen it for convenience. It wouldn't draw accolades from a man who owned ex-imperial palaces in his own country.

'Really.' A chuckle of approval rumbled up from the other man's chest. 'Your wife.' He nodded across the wide sitting room. 'She's a jewel of the first water. A rare find.'

Joss read the appreciation in Tevchenko's dark eyes and felt a scimitar-sharp slice of jealousy.

He froze, his coffee halfway to his lips.

Jealousy? Impossible.

Slowly he turned. He knew exactly where to find Leila. All evening he'd been aware of her—had felt an undercurrent of electricity running under his skin, tugging him like metal towards his magnetic north.

Leila had understood without being asked that she was to look after the wives and partners while Joss focused on business. She'd done her job brilliantly, allowing him to pursue his discussions without interruption.

She was a born hostess. She'd charmed even the most difficult. The secret, he'd discovered, was her genuine warmth. She took an interest in everyone she met.

With the exception of her husband.

She evinced no interest in Joss, keeping him at arm's length all week since those kisses.

It was frustrating. His heavy schedule and her reticence meant he was no closer to uncovering those secrets she hid so well.

Joss's eyes raked her. Tonight she was dressed modestly. No bare back to distract him. Yet in a slim-fitting dress of aquamarine she looked like a sea nymph rather than anything as prosaic as a wife. She wore her hair up, accentuating those flawless, high-cut cheekbones and the fragility of her long neck.

Just looking at her drove pleasure through him.

Beside her the trophy wives with their plastered-on dresses and tanned flesh looked garish and cheap, though their gems were probably worth the GDP of a developing country.

By contrast Leila wore a simple pendant that drew the eye to the delectable curve of her ripe breasts.

Joss frowned, realising it was the same pendant she'd worn each time they'd gone out. Did she wear nothing else?

'You don't agree?' the Russian boomed in his ear. 'As a new bridegroom I thought you'd be aware of your wife's special assets.'

Surely Boris wasn't crass enough to appraise her body so blatantly? Joss swung round, fury welling, his hands tight fists.

'She puts everyone at ease.' Tevchenko nodded to the women on the other side of the room. 'Even those two cats who were spitting and snarling at each other earlier.' He sighed. 'With a woman like that at my side...' He shrugged and grinned. 'I repeat, my friend. You're a lucky man.'

He clapped his hand to Joss's shoulder and Joss relaxed. He'd overreacted.

'I know.' Who'd have guessed Leila would eclipse his expectations? She was a valuable asset indeed.

Despite the inconvenient lust she inspired.

And the way she distracted him.

And the annoying way she was pointedly avoiding him after that taste of raw, mind-blowing passion.

It chagrined him that it was he who chafed at the restrictions of a paper marriage. He wanted more than a polite goodnight and a closed door.

His blood steamed, remembering how she'd brushed him off. It was only the shadows in her eyes that had convinced him not to press further.

But soon. Anticipation stirred in his belly.

As Joss watched, a newcomer, Asad Murat, joined her and the other women melted away. Joss's brow knitted. Leila's stance spoke of sudden tension, though he'd swear she hadn't moved a muscle.

He turned to the Russian. 'You'll excuse me?'

'Of course. If I'd married a woman like that I'd keep her close too.'

Joss made his way through the knots of guests to the far side of the room, curiosity rising. Leila stood, glass in hand, head tilted towards their guest as if eager to hear his every word. Yet some preternatural sense warned something was wrong.

He lengthened his stride.

'Am I interrupting?'

Murat started and took a step back. It was only then that Joss realised how close the pair stood. Leila turned smoothly, her smile perfect. Only the sharp glitter in her eyes confirmed Joss had been right. Something was up.

He reached out and slipped his hand through her arm. She stood stiffly, the pulse at her wrist racing.

'Not at all.' Leila's crystal-clear diction reminded him of her tone when she argued with him: polite, calm and with an undercurrent of acid. 'We were just discussing the importance of discipline.'

'Discipline?' Joss frowned. 'Self-discipline?'

Leila shook her head. 'The lack of it in modern society.'

Joss looked from one to the other, wondering what he'd interrupted. Leila was wound so tight it was a wonder her smile didn't crack. 'For example?'

When she said nothing, Murat took the lead.

'Society today is full of do-gooders carping about the weak and disadvantaged. They don't understand the strong in society need to take a lead, set an example.' He paused. 'Like us.'

'Us?' Joss had learned enough about Murat in this week's preliminary discussions to realise they had little in common except wealth and large-scale mining interests.

'Leaders. Strong-minded men. Men who aren't afraid to take a stand for what's right.'

Beside him Leila stirred, standing taller.

'I'm sorry,' Joss murmured, his eyes on Leila's white-knuckled hand gripping the stem of her glass. 'You'll have to be more specific.'

'A man needs to rule his home fairly but with a rod of iron.' The other man darted a look at Leila. 'And in commerce too. Take those labour problems you're having in Africa.' He expounded his theory on how that should be handled. With each sentence he confirmed himself totally devoid of anything like a social conscience, much less a scrap of humanity.

'An interesting approach.' Joss cut him off, disgust pungent on his tongue as he eyed the other man in disbelief. 'But not mine. You'll read in the news tomorrow that the strike has been settled. The conditions at the mine under the previous owner were archaic and brutal. From now on, as many local workers will be engaged as possible, after a full health and safety review. There will be new equipment and appropriate training for everyone on site.'

Joss paused, letting his words sink in. 'I've also offered

a profit-sharing incentive scheme in addition to plans to improve the fresh-water access and education of the local villages.'

'Are you mad? What about your profits?'

Joss stared into the other man's shocked face and realised he'd conned himself thinking he could ever do business with him. Ruthless he didn't mind. Hell, he'd been labelled that more times than he could count. But to exploit workers as virtual slaves as Murat suggested? The guy made him sick.

'Decent conditions and respect for workers increases productivity.' He curled his lips in a smile that showed his teeth. 'I recommend you try it before you're forced into it.' He paused. 'It's only bullies who can't respect the rights of others.'

Murat huffed and muttered then stalked away. Joss didn't bother to watch him go.

'Did you mean that?' Leila's lustrous eyes were huge as she looked up at him.

'Of course I meant it. He gives mining a bad name. One day there'll be a major disaster at one of his sites—a preventable disaster.' Joss paused, watching her closely. 'I know he's a family friend of yours but there's a limit—'

'He's no friend of mine!' She all but spat the words. 'I've spent the last five minutes gritting my teeth rather than tell him to leave and never come back.' Her brow knitted. 'I thought he was important to your plans?'

'No one is indispensable, Leila. Especially not him. I won't be doing business with him after all.' It was a decision he'd been considering all week. Tonight had just been the final straw.

Joss threaded his fingers through hers, feeling the tension thrumming through her. 'What did he say to you?' The waves of anger that had built as he listened to the other man swamped him.

'Nothing important.' Her gaze slid away and he knew she lied.

'Leila.' Joss slipped a warning finger under her chin and lifted her face. 'What was it?'

If the bastard had insulted her—

'Nothing worth repeating. Really.' She tilted her head, looking straight into his eyes as if trying to read *him*. 'Was that true? About your plans for the mine?'

'Yes. The deal just went through today.' He watched her arrested expression, wishing yet again he understood what she was thinking. 'Does it matter?'

Gravely she nodded. 'It matters.'

The slow curve of her lips was tiny, the barest hint of a smile, but it warmed him like sunrise in the desert, spreading heat in places that hadn't felt warmth in a lifetime.

Hours later Leila turned away as Joss closed the door on the last guest.

Tiredness caught her between the shoulder blades. It had been a stressful evening. She loved meeting new people but she was badly out of practice.

Time spent poring over papers and the Net couldn't make up for years cut off from news. All evening she'd wondered when she'd make some obvious gaffe, revealing how little she knew about what had happened in the world these last years when she'd been locked away.

Then there was Murat. Leila rubbed her hands up her bare arms, remembering the feral heat in his eyes as he'd cornered her.

'I'm tired,' she said to Joss over her shoulder. 'I'll go to bed now. Goodnight.'

She was at the entrance to the bedroom wing when his voice reached her. 'Not yet, Leila. We need to talk.'

Turning, she saw his stubborn expression. It had been there as he'd questioned her about Murat. Couldn't he let that rest?

She didn't like Joss getting too close. He made her feel things she had no business feeling, especially for a man who kept her purely for business.

Even a man who'd proved he was nothing like Gamil or his crony Murat.

Pleasure sang in her heart as she remembered Joss tonight, looking down his superb nose as he called Murat a bully. As he deliberately excluded him from a multibillion-dollar deal.

Joss, she realised, would never behave brutally like her stepfather. Despite his formidable power and strong will, *he* wasn't a bully.

He'd cared enough to worry about her health. He'd instructed his housekeeper to provide her favourite meals. He treated her with respect in front of others.

And when they were alone…heat washed her. Even when they fought, or kissed, he hadn't tried to force her.

That said everything about him. He was a man she could respect, maybe even like. It undermined her resolve to keep her distance and made her wonder about that lightning strike of passion. She'd never experienced anything like it. Maybe that was why she felt off balance.

She had so much to think about. She needed to be alone.

'I'm sorry, Joss. I'm exhausted. We can talk tomorrow.' Leila didn't wait for him to insist but walked down the hall to her bedroom. She felt tightly strung and hadn't the strength to face his probing.

She'd almost made it to her door when long fingers wrapped around her elbow, halting her.

Leila refused to think about how that warm grip sent ripples of sensation up her arm. How Joss's subtle spice scent brought back those heady moments in the lift when he'd taken her to the gates of paradise with his kisses and the press of his powerful body.

Heat scalded her cheeks as she swung to face him.

'We haven't finished talking.'

She arched her eyebrows. 'I told you I'm tired. We can talk in the morning.'

Her heart thudded once, twice, as she met his stare. Her chest grew tight as she held her breath, willing him to release her. She told herself he made her uncomfortable, invading her space. Yet it wasn't discomfort throbbing through her body.

'What are you frightened of, Leila? You can tell me.' His voice was deep and low, thrumming across her taut nerves. How could a man's voice feel like the stroke of velvet across her nape and breasts? Her skin tightened, her nipples budding as if from cold. Yet it was heat she felt, insidious heat that burrowed deep, deep inside.

'I'm not frightened.'

'No?' His dark eyebrows pitched down in a look of pure disbelief. 'Not even of our guest, Murat?'

'Him?' Leila's lip curled. 'He's a dreadful man but I'm not frightened of him.' Oh, there'd been a moment when they'd met again that had brought back in painful vibrancy all her stepfather had done, how he'd tried to reduce her to a shell of her real self. But tonight she'd felt only loathing.

In the dimly lit hall Joss stared. Why was he so persistent? He was the one who insisted they lead separate lives.

'If not Murat, then what are you hiding from?'

'I'm not hiding. Your imagination is running away with you.' Even as she said it, Leila knew it to be a lie. She longed for the sanctuary of her suite, away from Joss's piercing gaze. She didn't understand the warring emotions he evoked. His interest annoyed yet excited her.

She tugged her hand but he held her easily.

'If you're not hiding and you're not afraid, then you won't mind strolling with me out on the roof garden.'

Leila's skin iced.

'There's a marvellous view across the Thames and the scent of blossoms on the night air is magic.' He scrutinised her carefully. 'Out in the open we can get a breath of fresh air after that crush of people.' He paused. 'I understand you haven't been out there yet. Allow me to show you. There's a wonderful feeling of space and openness.'

Leila bit her lip, trying to stem rising panic. Space and openness... She shuddered, remembering how the sky had pushed down on her that day at the airport. Even going out with Joss in London in the safety of the limo had taken every ounce of courage. And the distraction of his kisses.

Her heart gave a nervous jolt.

He was waiting and there was something in his eyes that told her he understood her fear.

Her chin jerked up. Had he guessed? How?

Damn the man! Why couldn't he leave her be?

'If it's so important to you,' she said at last, her voice husky from her suddenly dry throat, 'do show me your roof garden.' She pivoted on her heel, determined to get this over with as quickly as possible. Surely she could manage just a minute or two. Surely!

'This way.' Joss pushed open a door and led her across a wide, carpeted room towards full-length windows. Beyond it Leila saw the outline of potted trees, a pergola, the shimmer of a delicate trail of water cascading artfully to a pool.

Her pulse rose to a clumsy gallop as she looked beyond and up to the wide sky that seemed to store and reflect the city's light haze. She imagined standing out there, under the weight of that vastness, and stumbled, catching her heel in the deep carpet.

Joss caught her to him, his heart a solid beat under her palm as she steadied herself. He reached out and slid open one of the glass doors.

Leila sucked in her breath, her eyes fixed on the movement. Cool air wafted in, brushing her goose-pimpled flesh. The muted sound of an ambulance in the distance echoed in her ears, mingling with the ebb and flow of her breathing.

Gritting her teeth, Leila moved away from Joss and took a

careful step towards the opening. She wobbled on the threshold and had to grab the door.

'Obstinate woman!' The words were a growl in her ear as Joss's arm wrapped around her waist, drawing her close.

She swung to face him.

'What do you *want* from me, Joss?' She couldn't hide the plea in her voice. Instantly pride came to her rescue. 'I told you I'm not afraid.'

'No?' Even in the semi-darkness she discerned the glitter of his eyes in that scowling face. 'You're running scared, Leila.'

She drew herself up, determined to keep her weaknesses to herself. They revealed too much she needed to keep private.

'What am I supposed to be running from?' If she had to she'd walk right across his precious roof terrace and lean out over the street below, rather than have his pity.

Even in the gloom she saw his jaw set hard.

'This.' It was a hiss of sound that barely reached her ears before his head obliterated the light and his lips took hers.

This time as his mouth crushed hers, something inside rose up to meet him. Something instantaneous and eager, hungry and desperate. Some animal instinct in her morphed out of fear and anger and the need that had been growing ever since Joss had held the wedding goblet to her lips and claimed her as his wife. Ever since he'd taken her in his arms and obliterated nerves and doubt and disquiet with the reality of his big, hard body and tender touch.

Leila melted, her knees giving way as she grabbed his shoulders with hard fingers.

'I'm not scared,' she whispered, her words muffled against his lips.

It was true. He was huge, powerful and strong, a dominant male. But she knew deep inside that Joss Carmody was a man unlike the one she'd learnt to fear. She clung tighter to his hard frame, feeling a tremor quake through him.

Joss made her feel…he made her feel…

Thought spiralled into nothingness as her senses took over.

'You should be scared.' Joss hauled her close, lifting her till their bodies were perfectly aligned. His long fingers spread over her bottom, holding her high and tight as he dragged his mouth from hers and rained hot kisses across her throat. 'You make me want to lose control.'

Leila's neck arched back under the weight of those brief, hard kisses that brought her body to tingling restlessness. She felt hot all over, shivering with it, yet craving the warmth of his body against hers as if her life depended on it.

She burrowed her hands in his hair, revelling in the thick softness against her fingers, cradling his head as he dipped lower, following the line of her necklace down between her breasts.

Liquid desire swirled and pooled low in her body, shocking her. It wasn't Joss losing control, it was her!

She should hate it. She should fear it. Surely losing control at his hands was to let him dominate as she'd vowed never to let him do?

Yet this felt glorious. It felt like victory, pleasure and power.

Joss lowered his head further and licked the line of her cleavage right up to the pearl pendant. He did it again, this time following the edge of her bodice high over her breast. Leila gasped as raw delight tore through every barrier she'd erected between them.

'You're totally in control,' she whispered, her voice a husky protest. She wanted him as helpless in the face of these overwhelming sensations as she. But she didn't have the experience to do it. All she had was instinct to guide her and Joss's undeniable expertise.

He looked up and she gulped, dry-mouthed, watching his tongue swirl anew over the side of her breast, feeling sparks of pleasure wherever he touched. She'd never known anything so erotic.

'You want to see me lose control?' Another swipe of his tongue, this time across the fine fabric of her dress till he found her nipple and bit gently through the fabric.

Leila's fingers dug into his scalp as her whole body jolted. Her eyes widened in shock as a low moan escaped her lips. Brazen excitement hummed through her. No thought of modesty or hesitation. She wanted Joss's touch on her. *She needed it.*

Her breath hissed between clenched teeth as she realised she teetered on the brink of giving herself to a man she'd known mere weeks.

'You don't want sex with your wife. You said so!' Was that her voice, that uneven whisper? Leila scrambled to straighten her body and her thoughts. This couldn't be happening.

But he held her tight so her wriggles only brought them into more intimate contact. Clamped against his erection, each movement was an erotic caress.

She stilled, horrified at how much she wanted to move against him.

'Oh, believe me, Leila, I do.' He ended the sentence solemnly, slowly, as if repeating the marriage vows they'd shared just weeks ago.

Valiantly she strove for sense.

'It's not in our agreement,' she gasped, telling herself to break his hold even as her hands cradled his head.

'Agreement be damned.' His mouth was at her throat again, each word planted against flesh that quivered at his touch. One large hand cupped her breast and she sagged in his embrace.

He swung her up as if she weighed nothing and whirled her away from the door.

A soft mattress took her weight as he crushed her beneath him. For a moment something like panic flared as his supe-

rior strength imprisoned her. Then he drew back, one hand
going to her hair, the other tracing her lips so tenderly she
had to work to repress a sigh of delight.

He wasn't forcing her. He was seducing her.

Leila waited for dismay to strike. It didn't.

'We can change our agreement, Leila.' His lips against her
ear had her arching up from the bed, senses on overdrive at
the unfamiliar touch.

'I want you, Leila. You want me. It's that simple.'

'How do you know I want you?' She put her palm against
his chest and pushed till he lifted his head. The dark shadows
emphasised the harsh planes of his features, their strength and
arrogance. His eyes glowed avariciously as he surveyed her,
as if anticipating the act of possessing her body.

Leila swallowed hard as anxiety pierced her.

Then she looked down to his taut mouth, saw what looked
like pain there. She heard his ragged breathing, so like her
own, and realised his heavy burden in holding himself in
check.

'Don't you?' His words were raw but his touch, one finger feathering her cheek then brushing her parted lips, was
gentle. Leila trembled at its devastating tenderness.

He heaved a deep breath. 'There's nothing wrong with
lust, Leila. Simple, straightforward physical need.' His lips
curved in a tight smile. 'You can't deny it's here between us.
It needn't change anything else.' He stroked her mouth again
and something unravelled inside her.

'Why not accept it? Enjoy it?' His low voice was deliciously persuasive. 'It won't go away no matter how much
you want to hide. Not till we've sated it.' His touch feathered
delight through her senses and despite herself, Leila revelled
in the hot weight of him holding her down.

Was that what she was doing? Hiding?

Leila tried to marshal her thoughts but Joss's touch, his

body, his breath on her face and the spicy male scent of his skin every time she inhaled made logic impossible.

'Enjoy it while it lasts, Leila. Then move on.'

Move on. She grasped at the words. He was right. She wanted to move on. Her plans for the future depended on her breaking away from Joss and standing on her own two feet. How could she do that when desire caught her in its silken net?

She looked up into dark, knowing eyes and realised he, with all his experience, understood this…conflagration of need far better than she.

Maybe it was her very inexperience that caught her out. She'd never kissed a man before Joss. No wonder her hormones ran riot. He touched her, the merest brush of one finger, and she went up in flames like a powder keg primed to explode.

Would this need haunt her till she gave in to it? How could she concentrate on her future while she fought this terrible longing for the man she'd married?

One taste of passion. Why not? One taste to satisfy the gnawing hunger. Then she could move on.

It sounded deceptively easy but at the same time inevitable.

Tentatively Leila lifted her hand to cup Joss's jaw, feeling the unfamiliar tickle of emerging bristles against her palm. He felt foreign. Unfamiliar. Wickedly attractive.

She slipped her hand into his hair and pulled his head down to hers.

CHAPTER NINE

WHAT HE'D DONE to deserve Leila in his bed, Joss didn't know. He *did* know she was different. This thing between them was different—more intense than anything he'd experienced.

Every touch, every look, grazed through the layers of familiarity, even boredom, that had accumulated after so many easy lovers.

This wasn't easy. This was heart-poundingly raw and hard and unfamiliar. He felt passion so potent it caught his throat as he stripped her dress to reveal the woman who'd haunted his thoughts.

His wife.

Was that why this seemed profound? Some remnant of primitive male instinct to possess *his* woman? Was that what invested her sleek, alluring body with such fascination?

His wife. His woman.

Joss shook his head. He didn't want to own her, just possess her long enough to find the mutual pleasure that had teased for weeks. He had no interest in a lifelong partner.

As for the tremor in his hands as he ripped open his shirt—eagerness, that was all.

His gaze raked her body, bare but for an innocent-looking cream bra and panties. He'd been wrong to worry she was anorexic. Slim, yes, delicate in a supple way that hinted at hidden strength, ripe in all the right places.

His heart hammered.

'Take your hair down.' The words grated as he wrenched out of his jacket and shirt together. Even the weight of air on his bare torso was heavy on sensitised skin. How would it be when Leila caressed him?

His gaze dropped to her sultry mouth as she reached to undo her necklace. He imagined her lips on his flesh, and his body spasmed tight in anticipation.

She dropped the pendant on the bedside table, drawing his gaze, reminding him of the need to grab the protection he kept close.

Abruptly he levered himself up, his mouth tightening in a crooked smile at her instinctive protest.

'Just for a moment, sweetheart.' Standing, he bent to kiss her stomach. The taste of her was addictive, and her scent, like sandalwood and sunshine, sent blood rushing urgently through his veins. He paused, swirling his tongue in her navel, biting a line of gentle nips down her flat belly to the top of her panties. He couldn't resist cupping her there, through the fragile fabric. She was hot and wet, pushing up against his palm with gratifying urgency.

'Soon,' he promised, planting a kiss where his hand had been and feeling her quake in response.

Joss fumbled with the rest of his clothes and the condom, hands shaking in his urgency. When he turned, her hair was spread wide around her shoulders, a ripple of voluptuous satin. Her eyes were huge in the moonlight, flickering down to his groin then back to his face.

That hint of trepidation would have been gratifying if he weren't so painfully aroused.

As it was he barely had the patience to strip her underwear without tearing it from her body. Then she was naked beneath him and he stilled in awe.

'You're more beautiful than I could have imagined.' He didn't recognise his roughened voice.

Leila shook her head, reaching for his shoulders and drawing him down to lie on her soft skin and slippery silk tresses. All his senses rioted as he pressed against her. Each harsh breath created friction that sharpened the tension, and when she slid her hands over his body…

'Yes, like that,' he growled, his voice a guttural whisper. 'Touch me.'

She was taking him to heaven. No, to purgatory, with those long, stroking caresses that ended too abruptly. With fingers that fluttered tentatively, then grasped firmly as they moulded and explored.

Joss moved his weight to one side, taking the opportunity to thrust her legs wider and sink between them. Her roving hands stilled and he grabbed one, anchoring it around his rigid shaft, his hand covering hers.

Was that a gasp? His hearing was clogged with his pounding heartbeat.

Her fingers twitched around him and his breath seared from his lungs. The feel of her there was almost too much to bear. And when she slid her fingers up, exploring, lightning flickered at the edge of his vision. He held her still, then guided her lower, gritting his teeth against the need to surge hard and high against her touch.

Too soon, he told himself, even as his buttocks tightened and his hips tilted urgently.

'Later,' he whispered, drawing her hand away and kissing her palm. She shivered as he laved the erogenous point on her hand, reminding him of how delightfully responsive she was.

That gave him the focus he needed to pleasure her instead of himself. At this rate his pleasure would come in an instant.

'Tell me what you like, Leila.'

Leaning down, he tasted her tip-tilted breast and heard her gasp. Gently he blew on her nipple, watching it bead for him.

'Tell me,' he demanded.

Her fingers burrowed in his hair, tightening as if to keep him there. 'Yes. That. I like that.'

'And this?' He turned to her other breast, one stroke of the tongue and then he held still, waiting.

'Yes!' She moved restlessly beneath him, her hands trying to drag him down to her breast.

'Say it, Leila.'

Her eyes flashed in the darkness. 'Kiss me there. Please, Joss.'

He rewarded her with a kiss and then opened his mouth to suckle her hard, revelling as she writhed beneath him.

He caressed her throat, the taut skin over her ribs, the soft flesh at her hipbone, with Leila's words soft music in his ears. 'Yes. There. Like that. Please!'

Every caress elicited a sigh, a ripple of tight pleasure and answering caresses of her own. By the time Joss reached her belly he'd never been so aroused.

He let his hand swoop low to her feminine curls and she arched against him.

Game playing could wait. Joss's control was at an end. Pushing her thighs wide, he palmed her bottom, tilting her pelvis.

'Yes?' He paused, needing to make sure.

'Yes.' Her soft sigh was an invitation to heaven.

Seconds later Joss did what he'd been craving from the first, one long, sure thrust deep and hard that seated him at her very core.

His skin prickled at that taste of rapture, his eyelids lowering the better to concentrate on the inconceivable pleasure assailing him. In the darkness he felt tight heat draw him down. Leila's fingers at his shoulders were a sharp reinforcement of pleasure so exquisite it bordered on pain. Was it like that for her too?

With a deep breath he opened his eyes and looked down. Her teeth were sunk into her bottom lip, her eyes closed and brow furrowed. The better to concentrate on pleasure or, it hit him, to stop a cry of pain?

Joss frowned. 'Leila?'

She didn't hear him, was lost in her own world. That he could understand. Tentatively he withdrew then surged again, watching her breasts wobble invitingly. Automatically his hand closed over one, a delicious, perfect fit.

Again he moved and the tension in her face eased. Her mouth sagged open in a soundless O of surprise.

He had the rhythm now, gentle at first, watching her eyes open and find his in dazed delight. With each measured movement the tension ramped up between them.

Still he moved slowly, trying not to rush her. She grabbed him hard and he heard breathless gasps as if the onslaught of pleasure caught her by surprise. She shuddered around him, her movements racking her whole body as ecstasy consumed her, her gaze holding his as if afraid to let go.

She tipped him over the edge. He let the dam wall of control shatter and spilled himself into her with a roar of rapture as the darkness collided with a sunburst of heat and power and unbelievable pleasure.

When Joss came to his senses he was draped over her, pushing her into the bed. His dazed brain scrambled towards sanity. Regretfully he rolled to his side, drawing her limp form with him. Her hair slithered between them, making him shiver as if he weren't sated to the core.

'Leila?' He squeezed her shoulder.

'Hmm?' She burrowed against him, all languid satiation. Joss grinned, his moment of doubt forgotten.

'Nothing.' He brushed the back of her head, letting his hand trail down her hair, swooping the curve of her back and bottom.

Heat stirred again in his groin and Joss froze.

Already?

Then his lips curved in a smile of masculine appreciation. Leila would kill him with her tempting body if he wasn't careful, but what a way to go!

Carefully he pulled back, gritting his teeth against the exquisite sensations, and slid from the bed, hauling up a sheet to cover her.

He strode to the bathroom and switched on the light, whistling between his teeth in anticipation at the thought of joining Leila again. Then he looked down to remove the condom and saw a smear of blood.

His easy satisfaction stripped away in a heartbeat. Frowning, he thought back to Leila's look of shock as they'd joined. The excruciatingly pleasurable tightness he'd encountered. The way she'd bitten her lip as if to hold back a cry.

Joss's breath hissed from cramped lungs.

Suddenly bedding his wife wasn't nearly as straightforward as he'd thought.

Joss's departure roused Leila from her dreamy state. Her body still vibrated with the echoes of pleasure. She thought she'd understood, or guessed, but nothing had prepared her for the reality of making love with Joss Carmody.

Was it always like this? This bliss so profound it stupefied?

Remembering snippets of past gossip she doubted it. She could only be thankful Joss had taken the time to make it good for her—make it wonderful. He'd been generous in a way she guessed not all men were.

Another point in his favour.

Leila smiled into the pillow that smelled of Joss and heat and something unfamiliar. Sex?

Her smile died as reality intruded. It had been sex between them and she knew what he expected of his bed partner. No strings. Short relationships. She shook her head, amending that to no relationships.

He wouldn't want her mooning over him just because they'd shared themselves. He'd talked of sating this lust and then moving on. Wasn't that what she wanted too?

A moment's hesitation horrified her into realising she

wasn't ready to move on from the bliss she'd found in Joss's arms. Not just the climactic pleasure, but the sense of oneness. She'd been alone so long, so very alone. That feeling of incredible closeness with Joss held an allure that beckoned her greedy heart. It was balm to the soul after the wasteland her life had been.

But she'd had her taste of pleasure. She wouldn't beg for more. Joss would be aghast if he guessed how much their union, that sharing of power, bliss and tenderness, had meant to her.

The bathroom door opened and Joss stalked into the room, backlit by a shaft of light. Leila's breath clogged at the sight of him, long, solid and moving with the easy grace of an athletic male in his prime.

She swallowed and told herself it was okay to eat him up with her eyes. It would be the last time she'd see him like this.

Her heart dived at the realisation.

He strode towards the bed, but instead of scooping up his clothes he stood, arms akimbo, staring down at her. She felt a blush rise to the roots of her hair and was glad for the sheet covering her.

'Goodnight, Joss.' She had to get the words out before her throat closed completely.

'Goodnight?' His eyes narrowed and she felt his scrutiny on her flushed face.

She dropped her gaze to the fuzz of dark hair across solid pectoral muscles, preferring not to meet his gaze.

'You said you don't sleep with your…with women.' She swallowed hard, digesting the fact she was now one of Joss's women and striving to squash the flare of jealousy she felt towards those nameless others. 'So I'll say goodnight.'

She pasted a smile on her face and made a show of plumping her pillow before lying down. As if she said goodnight to a lover every night and lay naked between the sheets, ignoring the way every slight movement teased her flesh with memories of his touch.

He didn't move. She frowned, finally meeting his eyes. He scrutinised her as if he'd never seen her.

'What's wrong?'

He shook his head. 'Nothing. But…' He paused and for a moment something like discomfort flitted across his features. 'How are you? Are you okay?'

Did he know? Had he guessed she'd been totally innocent, not even adept at kissing? Her cheeks turned fiery at the idea of him comparing her to his other women and finding her wanting.

'Never better.' She paused and realised it was the truth. Despite some stiffness, she felt marvellous. 'I'm ready for sleep. Goodnight.' Determined, she closed her eyes and tried to slow her breathing as if exhausted.

'Are you sure?' For the first time since they'd met Joss sounded tentative. So, she'd been that obviously inexperienced? Leila shrank inside.

'Really, I don't want to talk any more. Goodnight.'

Silence. No sound of him moving away.

'There's only one complication.' His deep voice curled around her like a caress. 'You're in my bed.'

Her eyes shot open and she surveyed the room. Horror filled her as she realised her mistake. She hadn't even noticed. She'd been totally swept up in passion.

Leila gripped the sheets in tense fingers. Now she'd have to leave the sanctuary of the bed and find her clothes under Joss's scrutiny. He mightn't feel embarrassed about his nudity but she wasn't used to showing herself to anyone. She bit her lip, acknowledging that just a short time ago she'd gladly bared herself to Joss. But that was in the heat of passion. This was different.

Taking a deep breath, Leila slid to the side of the bed. 'I'll go.'

But before she could get out Joss took the sheet from her and climbed in. Instantly Leila scooted away across the king-sized mattress.

'What are you doing?'

'Joining you.' He lay down, head on the pillow where she'd lain.

'But…you don't sleep with—'

'I thought you didn't want to talk? But if you'd prefer to chat…' He propped himself up on one elbow, watching her expectantly.

'No!' She refused to participate in a postmortem of what they'd done.

'Then close your eyes and go to sleep.' His voice dropped to a gentle note that made sensation ripple deep in her stomach. Longing? If she wasn't careful she could get used to his tenderness.

To stay here or to brave the open air? Leila told herself she had the guts to walk away, naked as the day she was born. After what she'd endured in the past, a few moments' discomfort was nothing.

But she *wanted* to stay. Foolish maybe, but she wasn't ready to walk away from Joss yet.

A wedge of fear lodged under her ribs, a presentiment of trouble. Leila ignored it and for once chose the easy path.

Silently she rolled away from him, drawing the sheet high.

For long moments she lay stiff and taut, straining to discern any movement. Joss said nothing and at last she began to relax.

Then an arm slid around her bare waist and drew her back against him.

'What are you—'

'Hush.' He settled her in the curve of his body, his hot flesh blanketing her. His hairy thighs tickled the backs of her legs and his powerful chest rose and fell against her back.

Fizzing excitement rose in her blood, a jitter of awareness that they were close enough to—

'I don't think this is a good idea.' She made to pull away but his arm at her waist prevented her.

When he spoke his lips were in her hair, his breath warming her ear. 'Just relax, Leila. Don't worry, I don't expect a repeat performance tonight.'

The stirring hardness behind her told a different story.

Contrarily his statement didn't reassure her. Why didn't he want her again? Had it been so very unsatisfactory? Leila blinked, dry-eyed, into shadows.

Had it been a mistake, succumbing to her feelings for Joss? Had it complicated her already difficult situation?

Leila had an awful feeling Joss's logic about giving in to lust to sate it was flawed. She felt she'd unleashed a genie, a strong, hungry, demanding force, that would be impossible to push back into its bottle.

'Relax, Leila.' His words drifted to her, deep and soothing, like the rhythm of his breathing and the gentle caress of his broad hand at her waist. 'Sleep.'

Since she and her mother had gone to live with Gamil, Leila had been a light sleeper, ever alert for subtle changes in atmosphere that might herald one of her stepfather's extreme mood swings. She knew she was too wound up to sleep, that it would take her hours.

Yet somehow that thought was the last thing she remembered before falling into deep, refreshing slumber.

CHAPTER TEN

JOSS INSERTED THE KEY that gave basement access to his private lift and waited impatiently for it to descend to him.

He'd left the office after one meeting and rejigged his commitments so he could return to the apartment mere hours after he'd left it.

His mind filled with a vision of Leila, sleeping in his bed, and a groan of pleasure escaped him. She was the problem, the reason he'd cut his work short.

A vigorous, healthy male, he'd had his share of women. But nothing had prepared him for the intensity of pleasure he felt with Leila. He couldn't put his finger on any one reason for it—her lithe, luscious body, her husky voice urging him on, the rich veil of her long hair that made her look mysteriously sexy and innocent at the same time. Her combative spark that urged him to provoke her. The fact that, even when she panted for his touch, he'd had to work to convince her to have sex with him. The look of wonder in her eyes as he'd brought her to climax.

The fact he'd been her first lover.

The embers of lust that had warmed his belly all morning burst into flame as he lingered on that thought. He'd never considered a woman's virginity until now. But Leila's reckless abandonment in gifting hers to him, the sheer beauty of watching her come alive for the first time ever to his touch, stole his breath.

He wanted more.

He'd been semi-aroused all night, sleeping with her yet determined to restrain himself when she was no doubt sore and stiff.

Joss had waited for her to wake this morning, eager to tempt her gently into pleasure. To his chagrin she'd slept soundly as he showered, shaved and loitered over his dressing, till he had no excuse to delay.

He'd revelled in the fact their lovemaking had knocked her out so completely. Yet he'd alternated between the desire to yank back the sheets and concern.

Concern. He didn't do concern. It was too…personal.

Yet, and it worried him to admit it, he spent more and more time thinking about Leila. Not simply as his hostess or partner in sex. But as a person.

He yanked his tie open. It choked like a noose, constricting his breathing.

Joss didn't get entangled with women. He was hard-wired to avoid it. He'd spent a lifetime shunning emotional ties and it was impossible he'd start getting wrapped up in them now.

No, this wasn't emotional. It was simple desire. Pleasure.

A noise roused him and he realised he'd been staring blankly into the open lift. How long had it been there waiting for him to step in?

Setting his jaw, he strode in and hit the button for the top floor. His image in the smoky wall mirror was grim. Joss wasn't surprised. He pulled his tie off and stuffed it into his pocket, then prised open the top buttons on his shirt, feeling marginally better by the time he'd stripped off his jacket.

Even after years in a suit he preferred to work in jeans, with his sleeves rolled up, out of doors.

But he wasn't working now. He'd come home to be with Leila.

He'd changed his work habits because of her.

Joss waited for anger to rise. Nothing came, not even annoyance. Instead of inconvenience it was pleasure he felt.

Last night they'd entertained in the apartment instead of an exclusive restaurant solely because of his suspicion that Leila had a problem leaving the premises. If someone had told him three months ago that he'd alter his plans for any woman, he wouldn't have believed it.

But last night had been an unrivalled success, providing the one-on-one time he'd wanted with key players in a relaxed environment. Leila, with her warmth and natural charm, had been a vital part of that.

The lift opened and he walked through the foyer and into the main sitting room.

He stopped. It looked…different. The ultra-modern designer he'd hired had favoured greys and black. Now it struck him that the room looked warmer than he remembered. Welcoming.

His gaze roved a low bowl of vibrant blooms, cushions in burnt orange and rust that softened the sleek lines of the leather sofa. There was a rug he'd only half noticed before, a swirl of colour that warmed the darker furnishings. A small, exquisite Art Deco bronze sculpture stood on an occasional table, its reflection clear in a nearby wall mirror that enhanced the light.

On the arm of a chair he saw a book, face down. He went over and picked it up. A recent political biography. Under it was a newspaper open at a section on university programmes and beneath that a glossy gardening magazine.

Hastily Joss put them down, feeling absurdly as if he'd intruded on Leila's privacy. He surveyed the room and it hit him what felt different. It felt lived-in. Like a home.

He stood, caught between horror and something like longing.

He'd never had a home in the usual sense. As an adult he'd been on the move too much to put down roots. As a child…

His mouth flattened. The places he'd lived as a kid had had none of the welcome he felt here. They'd been the scenes of too many emotional battles.

Joss looked around, telling himself a few ornaments didn't make a difference. It was window dressing. An illusion.

He turned on his heel and went looking for his wife.

His bed had been made—smooth and pristine as if he hadn't experienced the most climactic night of pleasure there hours before. He quelled disappointment. He hadn't really expected to find Leila there, waiting.

Movement outside caught his attention and he went to the sliding glass door that gave onto the roof garden.

His pulse thudded as he spied her in the shadow of the pergola. She wore slim-fitting jeans, a shirt of bright scarlet, and her hair was down, rippling loose to her waist. Joss's hands twitched as he recalled the feel of it in his fingers, its scent in his nostrils. In the sunlight it shone dark mahogany shot through with glints of russet.

He went to meet her.

Leila stood, head slightly bent, apparently grasping the back of a chair. He quickened his pace. This was the first time he'd found her outdoors by her own choice.

'Leila?' He halted behind her. The stiff set of her body made him pause instead of reaching to touch her.

'Joss.' She straightened but didn't turn.

'What are you doing?' He frowned. Had he been wrong then about her not wanting to leave the apartment?

She laughed, a short, harsh sound that grooved deep through his belly. 'Getting some fresh air.'

He closed the space between them till a mere hand span separated them. Tension radiated off her in waves.

'How long have you been out here?'

'Nine minutes.'

Nine. Not ten. A precise nine. He peered over her shoulder and realised she was staring at her watch. Timing herself?

Her hands were white-knuckled. His heart kicked hard against his ribs.

Joss reached out and brushed his hand down the dark glory of her hair. It was soft and sun-warmed but beneath it she shivered.

Hell! He'd been right. A turbulent roil of anger and anxiety filled his belly.

'Come on. Let's get you inside.' He closed in on her, bending to lift her into his arms.

'No!' She turned, gifting him with a view of stark eyes. She swallowed hard. 'Why do you always think I need carrying? I can walk.'

Before he could stop her she stepped past him. She moved like an automaton, stiff and jerky, but she walked. Even as he reached for her, instinct intervened and he dropped his hand. She didn't need him to carry her. Even if he wanted to. Nevertheless he shadowed her, a pace behind till she walked through the door he'd left open.

She stopped a couple of steps inside, breathing deeply. Behind her Joss snicked the door closed.

'Are you going to tell me about it?' No matter how often he told himself theirs was a business arrangement, Leila stirred protective instincts that had lain dormant since Joanna. The need to safeguard her was so strong it made a mockery of all he knew about himself.

'There's nothing to tell.'

So she was going to play it like that. Stubborn, independent woman!

If she wouldn't talk about that there was plenty more on his mind.

'Why didn't you tell me you were a virgin?'

She speared him with a glare. 'Why? So you could lower your expectations accordingly?'

Joss stared as her luscious mouth flattened in a mutinous line and couldn't prevent a bark of laughter.

Leila's hands went to her hips.

'Was I that amusing?'

Joss shook his head and took her hand. She tried to tug free but he held her easily. 'Warn me, don't you mean, to prepare for the most potent sexual experience I've ever had?' His thumb stroked her pulse point and he felt tremors race through her.

'There's no need to pretend.'

'You truly have no idea, do you?' He closed in so she was flush against him. Predictably she stood her ground, tilting her chin so she could watch him. 'What we shared, Leila—it was…' he sought words '…spectacular. Memorable.'

That was why he'd been preoccupied all morning. He let his finger trail from her palm up the inside of her arm to her elbow and saw her eyes dilate. Good. She felt it too, this powerful undercurrent between them.

Her cheeks coloured. 'Yes, you're very good at sex.'

'No, Leila, *we* were good together. *The two of us*. The chemistry is…explosive.' He paused. 'I just wish I'd known it was your first time. I'd have taken it slower and made it better for you.'

Her blush deepened to a delectable rose madder and she looked away. 'There was no need. I…enjoyed it too.'

Joss bit down the bubble of laughter that rose at her understatement. He'd watched her come apart beneath him, had ridden the lingering vibrations of her long climax and read the wonder in her eyes. 'Enjoyment' hardly covered what they'd shared. But he'd give her latitude since she was so inexperienced.

'I'm glad,' he murmured, lifting his hand to palm her cheek. Her skin was as soft as he remembered. His blood quickened. 'It will be even better next time.'

'Next time?' Leila's voice was unsteady. 'You said we'd get it out of our systems. Enjoy it then move on.'

It struck Joss that for all her fiery spirit and stellar social skills, Leila was incredibly naïve about what went on between a man and a woman. He drew a deep breath. He looked forward to teaching her.

Joss wrapped his other hand around her waist, drawing her up to feel his arousal. Surprise crossed her face and a fleeting instant of furtive feminine pleasure.

Oh, yes, he was going to enjoy this thoroughly.

'And so we will move on.' He lowered his mouth to her neck, inhaling the scent of sandalwood and sweetness. 'After we've had our fill.' He planted a kiss beneath her ear and revelled in her quiver of response. She lifted her hands to his chest and his heart pounded. 'But it will take some time to reach that point.'

'I see.' Her words were a soft exhale. Her hands crept up his shoulders and Joss smiled.

'Until we reach that point I suggest we enjoy it.'

Leila leaned back in his arms, her eyes more pewter than green as she surveyed him intently. 'But no strings?'

Joss frowned. *She* asked for no strings? That was a turnaround. It was usually him insisting on independence while women wanted more. For some reason that niggled at him.

'Absolutely.' His mouth hovered over hers. 'Simple mutual pleasure.' After all, he didn't know any other way.

Simple? There was nothing simple about what she shared with her husband.

Leila lay under his massive form. Her breath came in desperate gasps, aftershocks of bliss rippled through them and she knew with absolute certainty that sex had complicated their relationship.

But she couldn't regret it.

Her chest constricted on a surge of emotion as she palmed the damp luxury of his back and felt his growl of approval reverberate through her. She'd never known such wondrous pleasure. They were joined, were still one, and, no matter how hard she tried to deny it, the feelings that evoked were profound. Peace. Pleasure. Trust.

Would it be like that with another man? Was this what any woman felt with her first lover or was there something special about Joss? Without words, with the gift of his passion he'd reached deep inside her to emotions she'd repressed and drawn them to the surface.

In the last weeks Joss had ceased to be a stumbling block to her new life. He'd become vital to it.

That scared her. Her strength came from self-reliance. She couldn't afford to need anyone, especially not the man who'd chosen her for the commercial benefits she brought.

'Back in a moment,' he murmured and rolled away, heading for the bathroom.

Leila sighed, telling herself it was relief she felt being alone, not regret. Yet her arms were empty without him and the bed cold.

Annoyed with herself, she rolled away. She'd been caught up in the glamour of receiving Joss Carmody's full attention and the sensual onslaught of his lovemaking. She shivered and drew the sheet tight around her. He made her feel as if she were the only woman in the world, the only woman who mattered.

Did all his lovers feel that way or was that a sign of her inexperience?

For a moment there she'd felt something so profound it was hard to believe it wasn't real and permanent.

The bed shifted as he got in, reaching for her. Leila stiffened. She should move away, assert herself instead of succumbing to his touch. But her body had other ideas. Already she was snuggling close as he settled her against his shoulder.

'Are you going to tell me now?'

'Tell you what?' Her breath caught as his hand circled lazily along her ribs and grazed her breast.

'About the roof garden. What you were doing, timing yourself.'

'You said there'd be no strings.' Leila fought to inject power into her voice as her body softened like sun-warmed chocolate at his touch. 'I don't have to answer questions.'

'No, you don't. But I'm…' he paused so long she wondered if he'd continue '…concerned about you.'

There it was again, that fillip of sensation at the idea someone cared. That *Joss* cared.

Did it take so little to winkle out the weakness she'd striven so hard to hide? A weakness revealed was a weakness to be exploited. She'd learned that from Gamil.

'There's no need to be concerned. I'm fine.'

'That doesn't answer my question.'

Leila braced herself against his chest, trying to rise. His arm wrapped around, holding her close. She tried not to enjoy the feel of his hot, bare chest beneath her cheek.

'Why do I have to tell you anything? You never tell me about yourself.'

Her curiosity about the man she'd married grew daily. Instead of a brash, bossy, self-important tycoon, Joss had proven himself not only intelligent and with a keen nose for business but affable, sexy and *likeable*. Initially he'd angered her with his demands and the assumption she'd starved herself deliberately. But these past weeks she'd come to enjoy his company. Though she was a trophy wife he somehow made her feel *more*, as if he truly valued her, as if he cared for her well-being, even her opinions.

'All right, then. Answer a question of mine and I'll answer one of yours.' He stroked the underside of her breast and she shivered. She tried to summon anger that he used her response to his touch against her, but it was delight she felt, not annoyance.

'Tell me why you dislike Murat so much.'

The question took her by surprise. She'd expected him to

ask about her fear of going out. She was almost certain he'd guessed it.

'And then you'll answer my question?'

'Cross my heart.' Yet it was the upper slope of her breast that he crossed with his index finger. When he'd finished his hand trailed provocatively to her nipple, awaking every nerve in a clamour of sensual delight.

Leila grabbed his hand and clamped it at her waist. He wouldn't have this all his way.

'I dislike Murat because he reminds me of my stepfather. They're two of a kind and I despise them both.'

A charged silence followed her words. Leila could almost hear Joss digesting that and considering its ramifications.

She was breathing hard and fast, her grip on Joss's hand vice-like with the strength of her feelings. Deliberately she lifted her hand away but had nowhere to plant it but his broad chest. That was solid beneath her touch, wiry hair tickling her palm, the even thud of his heart calming after her rush of emotions.

Before he could question, Leila spoke again. 'Why do you want a business arrangement instead of a real marriage? A wife for show, not a real one? And no children, no family?' It had puzzled her ever since she had realised Joss wasn't the cold tycoon she'd imagined. 'Most people want love, belonging, children.' Leila paused, realising suddenly how much she asked. No doubt he'd avoid answering.

'Remind me to think twice about negotiating with you again.' His deep voice held reluctant admiration and humour. She imagined that sexy half-smile grooving his cheek.

'You won't tell me?' She ran her fingertip over his chest, watching his nipple harden intriguingly as she circled it. His hand caught hers, imprisoning it flat against his chest.

'I left myself wide open, didn't I?' His other hand stroked her hair and she tilted her head into his touch.

'How can you want something you've never known or

seen?' he said at last. 'I know there are people who swear their family life is wonderful, but I suspect they exaggerate.' He breathed deep. 'I'm not stupid enough to put myself in a vulnerable situation where some woman has the power to make a fool of me when I discover we're all wrong for each other.' He shrugged. 'Not that it would happen. No woman has ever tempted me to consider a long-term relationship.'

Leila digested that. 'You're scared to trust?'

His hand tightened on hers. 'Not scared. Just understandably doubtful.'

'Because you don't trust women?' He wasn't a misogynist. His attitude surprised her.

'Because I've seen how destructive families can be, especially for kids.' His voice was grim. It tugged something deep inside her and she turned her head, pressing her lips to his chest in a gesture of sympathy. Whatever had happened in his childhood it had scarred him.

'You don't need to feel sorry for me, Leila.' Yet his palm caressed the back of her head as if to keep her close. She breathed deeply of his intriguing, masculine scent.

'I know.' He was big and tough and in control of his life— well able to take care of himself.

Yet even she, after Gamil's brutal treatment, held out hope of trusting a man with her happiness one day. She had her parents' example as a model and not even the last years had extinguished her belief in the power of love.

What was it like not having hope to hang onto? She slid her arm around his torso, hugging him, and his hand settled in her hair.

'I'm sorry your childhood was hard,' she murmured.

'Yours wasn't?'

She shook her head. 'Oh, no. Mine was sunshine and laughter and lots of love. My parents adored each other and made me feel special every day of my life.' She'd never imagined telling Joss any of this, but the words slipped out easily. 'I was very lucky.'

'You were.' His deep voice held a new note. 'My earliest memory is of my mother screeching abuse and the sound of china smashing.'

'She was violent?' Leila shuddered, burrowing closer.

'Only with breakables.' His tone was sardonic. 'My mother made her point with maximum drama when she didn't get her way. As her expectations exceeded her income and her vanity, that was often. My father, on the other hand, specialised in aloof disapproval. He'd cut anyone down to size with a few words.' He paused. 'One passionate, the other cold, both focused on themselves. They should never have had a child, much less two.'

'You have a sibling?'

The hand stroking her hair stilled and the fine hairs at her nape prickled.

'Had. Joanna died when I was ten.'

'I'm sorry, Joss.' She hadn't meant to cause pain. 'An accident?'

'For someone who doesn't want to talk about herself, you ask a lot of questions.'

It was true. The depth of her curiosity surprised her.

She lifted her head. His eyes glowed dark indigo and his face was pared to stark, powerful planes. Deep lines bracketed his mouth. Fellow feeling welled up inside her. She wanted to wipe his hurt away, give him ease.

'I'm sorry,' she said again.

'It's okay, Leila.' His lips quirked. 'Don't look so worried. It's all in the past.'

She shook her head. 'Some things stay with you.'

His smile faded and he gathered her close.

'You're right. I'll never forget Joanna and what she went through. Our parents made her life hell, pulling her between them. Six months in England with our mother, being taught society ways, then six in Australia, berated for being too delicate instead of athletic and academically gifted. Her life was a struggle to conform to what *they* wanted. They played out their feud using her as a pawn. Never once did they think about what *she* needed.'

Leila noticed he talked about his sister, not the impact his parents' feuding had on him.

'By the time she was thirteen she was depressed. At fourteen she was severely anorexic.'

Leila gasped. Now it made sense—his accusations about her weight loss. He hadn't just been crass, but genuinely worried. 'So that's why—'

'It seemed possible,' he said flatly. 'I'd seen it before.'

'What happened to her?' Leila's throat dried.

'She ran away at fifteen and I never saw her again.' His voice was empty. 'When my mother told me she'd died of her illness she tried to make me believe it was because Joanna had been selfishly wrapped up in herself rather than caring about *her* like a daughter should.'

Leila propped herself up. 'That's outrageous!' What a thing to say to a grieving little boy.

'That was my mother, generous to the bone.' He shrugged. 'I've seen too much of dysfunctional families to want another. I'm alone and that's how I like it. I'll never bring a child into this world to suffer because its parents grew to hate each other like my parents. Even on opposite sides of the world they fought their petty battles through us. The last thing I want is children. My family genes aren't something I want to pass on.'

His mouth tightened and she read grim intent.

Now the terms of their prenup made sense. No real marriage. A penalty for pregnancy. Joss used the law to cut himself off from any chance of a family.

Her heart went out to him. He had it all socially and financially yet she grieved for the vacuum at his heart where

love should be. He'd probably call himself self-contained.
She thought it tragic.

His gaze clashed with hers. 'I don't want sympathy. It's
wasted. I didn't tell you so you'd feel sorry for me, but so
you'd understand I'm serious about no long-term emotional
involvement.' His gaze shifted, dropping from her face, and
his expression took on a saturnine cast that skimmed something almost like fear through her.

'But there's something else you can give me.' He cupped
her breast, not gentle this time, but purposeful. His fingers
pinched her nipple and she gasped as pleasure teetering exquisitely close to pain shafted through her. Involuntarily her
body curved into his.

His smile was wolfish, past hurt buried behind a visage
of hungry lust.

'That's what I want, Leila. Sex. Simple physical pleasure.
Can you give me that?'

His eyes glittered and she felt a tide of answering hunger
engulf her. The passion they'd unleashed was primitive and
unstoppable. Yet that didn't prevent her seeing the shadows
in his eyes, the hurt buried deep. Her heart squeezed hard
for all he'd endured.

So when he grabbed a condom then tipped her onto her
back she didn't object. He pushed between her thighs, suck-
ling hard at her breast and she gathered him close, giving herself up to his need. He touched her between her legs, probing
her readiness, and she arched into his hand, eager to give him
the sweet oblivion he craved.

When, moments later, he thrust in hard and sure, his hands
unyielding on her hips, his face stern with the force of his
need, Leila gave herself willingly. And when he shuddered
to a climax that pumped on and on, his hoarse shout echoing
in her ears, Leila tugged him to her, cradling him with all
the tenderness that welled up inside her.

CHAPTER ELEVEN

AFTER THAT JOSS ASKED no more questions. Since revealing his troubled past he avoided anything personal.

Personal except for their ardent lovemaking every night and morning. And now he'd taken to coming back to the apartment for lunch.

The first day he'd arrived as Leila was finishing laps in the indoor pool. She still blushed to think of what they'd done on the wide lounger by the water. She'd been utterly abandoned, giving herself up to the spiralling whirlwind of desire that grew daily rather than abated.

A flicker of anxiety stirred. It didn't *feel* as if this was the way to get rid of her physical weakness for Joss.

If anything, she turned to him more, enjoying the evenings when, instead of working or entertaining, Joss joined her to listen to music or watch a DVD. Intimacy wasn't just about skin-to-skin contact, but precious shared peace.

That she'd found it with her husband of all men stunned her.

Perversely, the fact he no longer pressed her for information made her wonder if she should trust him with the truth.

He must have guessed some of it. Though he said nothing, every time they went out he gathered her to him in the lift and kissed her till her head spun and her nerves vanished. When the limo threaded busy city streets, Joss would clamp her to his side and distract her with conversation or, more often, his marauding touch. Now she almost looked forward to going out.

She'd given up worrying that she emerged from the car dishevelled. Joss declared he preferred her looking sultry and hot rather than buttoned up and cool.

Maybe he was just boosting her ego. Unlike Gamil, who'd made it his mission to destroy first her mother then her, Joss made her feel good. He valued her contribution to his commercial schemes and said so. And when they were alone and naked, the sound of his praise always filled her with delight. He made her feel wonderful: sexy and strong.

Had he any idea how much that meant?

Leila slid a look at Joss beside her in the restaurant alcove. Each day she expected to discover he'd diminished, that the glamour that drew her to him wore off. If anything he looked more charismatic and potently masculine.

As if attuned to her thoughts, Joss slid his hand to hers, tracing a finger up her arm till he reached her sensitive inner elbow and she shivered. Instantly he smiled, his hooded eyes giving a glimpse of ravening hunger she knew no meal could sate.

A trickle of excitement slid low as his smile widened.

Sex, that was what he was thinking about.

Yet he hadn't needed to bring her out to lunch every day this week if he'd just wanted sex. She was so blatantly eager for his touch they both knew she'd give him what he wanted the moment he entered the apartment.

Nor was he here to network. They were seated away from the windows in a quiet, exclusive corner.

Now she thought about, it they were always seated well inside any venue. Deliberately?

Slowly Leila put her knife and fork down, reviewing the past weeks. The occasional outings had become more frequent. Her nerves had stretched that first time when the city had seemed vast and threatening. Joss never gave her time to worry or back out, simply appearing and announcing they were going to lunch. He kept her close, distracted by conversation and his blatantly sensual caresses.

Her eyes rounded as she digested details she'd not taken time to consider before.

Her progress in venturing out wasn't all down to Joss. She forced herself outdoors every day, starting with a few minutes on the roof garden and short expeditions to the building's foyer and onto the street.

But with Joss she'd managed to do so much. With Joss the fear faded into a mere prickling undercurrent.

'Leila? What is it?' The lustful glint in his eyes dimmed and concern replaced it.

That was when she knew.

Joss had no need to take her out. With his wealth he could bring in the best chefs to cook for him.

This was about *her*.

Leila's head spun.

'You've brought me out to lunch every day this week.'

Joss looked into green-grey eyes turned mysteriously smoky and wished again that he could read his wife better. Some things, like her desire for him, were easy. But always he sensed she hid so much.

It shouldn't matter. Yet he couldn't quench his need to know.

'You don't enjoy yourself?' He frowned. *He'd* enjoyed spending time with a woman who was every bit as fascinating as he'd suspected.

'Of course.' She gestured abruptly. 'But you're giving up your work time. You even come home early at night.'

Home. There it was again, that word filtered into his subconscious again and again when he was with Leila.

Returning to her felt like coming home.

Joss frowned and swallowed a mouthful of Chablis. His

gazed dipped to Leila's kissable mouth and his muscles tightened in ready arousal. He…appreciated Leila but that was as far as it went. He didn't need her.

'You're afraid I let my responsibilities slide?' He tried to tell himself she worried about whether that would impact his profits and her allowance, but it didn't work. Leila no longer convinced as a money-hungry gold-digger. That woman had been a mirage.

'I know what you're doing, Joss.'

His gaze rose to her eyes, lustrous and huge. When she looked at him that way his chest tightened and he had trouble marshalling his thoughts.

'What am I doing?' The words emerged gruffly. 'Spending time with my bride is hardly a crime.'

Yet he bluffed. Deep within he felt something akin to embarrassment at how much pleasure he took in her company. Never had he enjoyed a woman outside bed as much as he did in it. It was a first. One he preferred not to examine. Better to accept and enjoy the unexpected bonus marriage had brought then move on.

'You're not doing this just because you want to.'

Joss swallowed the betraying truth that his choice to be with her was utterly selfish. Just watching her lips move, hearing her husky tones, knowing soon she'd be in his arms, was pure pleasure.

'You know, don't you?'

Something in her voice dragged him out of his reverie. Leila looked—defeated.

He snagged his hand around hers where it rested on the table. Instantly a frisson of electric energy sizzled under his skin. Normally it disturbed him—that charge for which there was no rational explanation. Now he ignored it, too intent on Leila.

'What are you talking about?'

Her lips twisted in a travesty of a smile and she darted a look at the plate-glass windows across the room.

'That I'm…anxious about going out.' Her words were soft, as if she didn't want him to hear, but her chin tilted regally and she swung round to meet his gaze with a stoic pride that squeezed his chest.

Joss's fingers meshed with hers. 'I guessed.' At first it had been hard to believe—that a woman as sassy and strong as his bride should harbour such fear, but the evidence had built inexorably.

'You haven't asked about it.'

He shrugged. Of course he wanted to know. But after revisiting his own troubled past, his desire to push her into telling him had waned. Her desperate pride struck him as precious and hard won. Who was he to strip that away?

Carefully he weighed his words. 'I'm interested, of course.'

'Because you don't want a defective wife?' Her bite of self-derision told him how much she abhorred what she saw as a weakness.

He slid his fingers over hers, as if his touch could soothe. He, who had no skills in caring for anyone!

'I owe you an explanation, I suppose.'

She looked as if she faced a firing squad, drawn up tight and proud. A better man would assure her he didn't need to know her secrets.

But Joss had never thought himself a better man in anything other than wheeling and dealing, and getting whatever he wanted.

He wanted to understand.

Leila looked down at his hand covering hers. 'It happened first the day of the wedding.'

'Not before?' His gut clenched. She couldn't mean marrying him had caused her fear!

But already she was shaking her head. 'Never before.' She

paused and the taut silence stretched every nerve into jangling discord.

'When the car drew away from the house I was nauseous, wobbly as if I'd eaten something that disagreed.' She swallowed convulsively. 'When we got to the airstrip…'

Leila shook her head. 'I'd never felt anything like it. It was as if the weight of the sky crushed me, pushing the air from my lungs so I couldn't breathe.' Her breasts rose and fell as her breathing grew choppy. 'It all seemed so huge, so limitless, so frightening.' Her voice faded on a gasp that rattled in her chest.

Joss wrapped his other arm round her and drew her to him along the banquette seat. She sat stiffly. She didn't even seem to register his touch and Joss wondered if he should have deflected this discussion. But selfishly he waited for enlightenment.

When she continued it was in a breathless voice that didn't sound like the proud woman he knew.

'I thought myself strong. Even fighting a battle I couldn't win I never gave up. But when the threat is on the inside…' She swallowed hard, as if forcing down rough shards. 'These last years, even on the worst days I refused to admit defeat. But this—' She shook her head and a lock of hair tangled over her shoulder, an unwinding skein of mahogany silk. Joss chafed her hand, stunned at how it had chilled. 'I thought I was going to die.'

'I wouldn't let you.' He didn't formulate the words. They simply emerged. But they were true.

Her lips pulled in an uneven smile that spoke of pain. 'You distracted me enough to stop me giving in to it. Thank you.' Her eyes met his and again that electric spark hit him. This time it jagged deep into his vitals.

'Why? Do you know what brought it on?'

Leila shifted straighter, tugging her hand from his. Inexplicably he felt…deprived.

'I—' Her tongue flicked out to moisten her lips as she stared towards the window and its view of bustling London. 'I suspect it's because I wasn't used to going out.'

Joss waited. The pressure of expectant silence would draw the truth better than any encouragement.

'My life before this wasn't…normal.'

Joss watched her skin draw tight over her finely moulded features and fought the urge to ask. She said this had started on their wedding day yet she'd spoken about the last few years as if they'd been a battle. Tension screwed every muscle. He had a dreadful pit-of-the-belly premonition he wasn't going to like what he heard.

'Didn't you ever wonder why I married you?' Her gaze flicked to him.

He shrugged, about to say he'd assumed it was for wealth and position—what women always wanted. He'd learned that early from his dear mother. But since coming to know Leila, he'd learnt neither of those topped her list of desires.

Why hadn't he bothered to find out?

Because he didn't want to delve too deeply?

Her eyes bored into his. 'I would have married *anyone* if it meant escaping. No matter how unappealing.'

Leila found him unappealing? She had a fine way of showing it. Yet the bone-shivering urgency in her voice extinguished Joss's instant outrage.

'Tell me.'

She held his gaze so long he wondered if she'd speak again. Finally she dipped her head to look at her hands, twisted together on the table.

'My mother was a beautiful woman. Not just pretty but vivacious, the sort who drew admiration without trying.'

It didn't surprise him. Her daughter was the same. Leila had a special quality, not mere beauty or charm or even spirit, but a combination of the three that spotlighted her in any crowded room. It tugged at him like an inexorable tide.

'After my father died Gamil courted her. He was always there, wherever she was. He was charming, eager to please and devoted.' Yet Leila's voice was flat as she spoke. 'Eventually my mother agreed to marry him. It wasn't a love match like her marriage to my father, but he seemed a good man and she wanted me to have someone other than herself to rely on.'

Leila bit her lip so hard Joss feared she'd draw blood. But as he reached out she spoke again. 'It turned out Gamil wasn't the model husband she'd thought. What he called love was really obsession. Once they married he grew increasingly possessive and controlling, needing to know where she went, who she saw. He was pathologically jealous.'

Eyes the colour of a storm cloud met his and any idea she exaggerated died at the wretchedness Joss read there.

'He called her a whore. Accused her of being unfaithful. Accused her of bringing me up to be the same—weak, corrupt and licentious.' Lightning flashed in her eyes. 'My mother was *nothing* like that!'

'Of course not.' If she had been, Leila would have been different, not the wife who bedazzled him with her spirit and unshakeable honesty. The memory of the night she'd given him her virginity still had the power to suck the air from his lungs.

Joss's skin prickled at the idea of her being at the mercy of such a man. He didn't question her story. His wife was secretive but she wasn't a liar.

'Gamil was unhinged. I'm sure to anyone outside the house he appeared normal. But inside it was different. The restrictions tightened one by one. First the Internet stopped working. Trouble with the connection, he said, but he'd cancelled it. Then the phone. There were limitations on where we went. My mother's servants were dismissed on various pretexts and replaced with his own—people who'd spy for him. People who'd tell him what he wanted to hear.' She drew a deep breath. 'By the time my mother succumbed to cancer he'd broken her spirit and her will to live.'

Joss's skin iced as the implications sank in. 'You were alone with him then?'

'Except for his servants.' Her bitter tone told him they'd been no protection.

'He hurt you?' Joss leaned forward, his hand hovering over her taut fists. He remembered the livid bruise on her wrist, and red mist rimmed his vision. If he'd known this when the bastard had toadied to him—

'Not physically.' Yet she rubbed her hand absently over her arm. 'He had other ways.' Again Leila looked towards the restaurant's full-length windows and her expression made his belly clench.

'Gamil kept me prisoner after Mum died. I'd started a university course but deferred it when she got ill. He informed the university I wouldn't return.'

'Why did you let him?' Disbelief rose in him. Leila always stood up for herself. It was one of the things he admired even though initially he'd found her feisty attitude annoying.

She laughed. He didn't like the humourless sound.

'In Bakhara a guardian has complete control over his daughter, or stepdaughter: where she lives, where she goes, who she sees. That lasts until she turns twenty-five.'

'Or until she marries.' It was a guess, but it explained why she'd marry a stranger when she needed neither wealth nor social standing. What she must have suffered! The thought of Leila so desperate and defenceless made him feel sick with thwarted fury. How he wished Gamil were here right now.

Her eyes lifted and her lips curved in a tight smile. 'I always knew you were clever.'

Something sliced through his belly like a hot blade. Horror at her story? Regret that she'd come to him out of desperation? Guilt that he'd married her without bothering to find out why?

What sort of man was he, so self-important that he'd accepted without question that any woman would want him?

He looked at her wry smile, her proud chin and shadowed

eyes and knew she was strong in ways he'd never had to be. He felt pride, pleasure and gratitude that she was his...for now.

'You couldn't get away?'

Her mouth pursed. 'I tried. Several times. But I didn't get far. The law was on his side and I had no money, nothing but the clothes I stood up in. I couldn't go to my friends for help. Those would be the first places he'd look. He even brought the police in to search—saying I'd been kidnapped!'

'So he kept you in the house.' No wonder she'd called herself a prisoner. He'd seen the house. It was old and rambling, with several courtyards, but he couldn't imagine being locked up there. 'How long?'

She shrugged. 'Two years, more or less.'

'Two years?' Shock reverberated in his voice. 'Surely...' He shook his head, trying to process that it was possible in this day and age.

'I know.' Her voice grew husky and her gaze slid away. 'I should have found a way to escape for good, even with his guards and the police on his side. But each time it got harder, the punishments harsher.'

'I thought you said he didn't hurt you?' Joss's hand clenched on the back of the seat but he resisted the urge to embrace her. She sat rigidly as if there were a 'Do Not Touch' sign emblazoned across her.

'Not physical violence. But one by one he removed what he called my *privileges*. There was no phone or Net. I couldn't go out and there were no visitors, not even my few distant family members. Finally he cancelled the newspapers and removed the books.' Her eyes lifted to his. 'We had a library of books, some hundreds of years old, collected by my family. They vanished overnight.'

Her hollow tone tore at Joss. He thought he'd known dysfunctional relationships, but Gamil could have taught even his parents.

'All the servants changed, even the cook who'd been with us for years. No mirrors—'

'No mirrors?'

'They encourage vanity and licentiousness.' Leila gave him a straight look. 'I told you he was unhinged. My mother's jewels disappeared. He only gave me back the pearls so I could impress you and he kept the money that should have been mine.'

Joss swallowed hard. He remembered how she wore that pendant again and again. She'd clutched the pearl bracelet the day he'd threatened to return her to Bakhara if she reneged on their agreement. Ice slid down his spine as he recalled the pearls scattering across the floor as shock froze her face.

Why hadn't she *told* him?

Even as he thought it the answer came. After years of abuse why should she trust a stranger? A male stranger. One who had done business with her dreaded stepfather. Joss reviewed his actions from Leila's perspective and his pride shrivelled. Had she thought him as odious as Gamil?

He felt physically ill, rejecting the comparison with every cell in his body.

Whatever her first impressions, Leila trusted him now. She'd trusted him with herself, with her virginity. It struck him that she opened herself to him now with an honesty beyond anything he'd experienced with anyone.

Her trust and strength humbled him.

'After my last escape I was confined with bread and water in a storage room. That was what scared me most.'

'That's why you were so thin at the wedding?' The truth hit him with a crippling blow. 'You'd been starved?'

'Shh.' Leila looked around the restaurant but it was late and they were seated far from the rest of the diners. The staff kept their distance, respecting Joss's earlier request for privacy.

'Leila—tell me.' He grabbed her hand, feeling the supple warmth of her grip, assuring himself she was recovered.

'Not quite starved.' Her tone was bitter. 'I had to be well

enough to marry. Gamil is ambitious and wants to leverage his position at court using your status.'

'I played into his hands.' It didn't matter that the deal they'd struck gave Joss everything he'd wanted. He felt dirty, knowing he'd aided Gamil's schemes.

'It doesn't matter.' Her fingers threaded his. 'Because of you I got away. I escaped.'

At what price? Married to a man she'd never wanted. Terrified to go out.

'Don't look like that,' she whispered. 'You'll scare the waiters.'

He looked into her bright eyes and wondered how she'd endured without giving up. 'Tell me about the room where you were kept.' He had to know it all.

She blinked but didn't look away. 'It was small. Just large enough to lie down. It had a high window that let light in but had no view.' She paused. 'It was a little bigger than the lift to your apartment.'

Joss's breath hissed from his lungs. He'd been right about her terror. But he'd never imagined anything like this.

'No wonder you didn't want to go out.'

Her taut smile tugged at his heart.

'Pathetic, isn't it? The day I left home in Bakhara it suddenly struck me how big and dangerous the outside world was. How safe I was inside. Safe!' She shook her head. 'If it wasn't funny it would be heartbreaking.'

Joss saw the self-disgust in her face and knew it *was* heartbreaking. That Leila had had to endure this. That even now she seemed to blame herself in some way.

He'd never felt such a connection, an awareness of another's vulnerability, since Joanna. Yet this was different. It was more than pity and fear. There was admiration and much more—emotions he couldn't name. They churned inside like a curling wave smashing down on the shore.

'You're a remarkable woman, Leila.'

Startled, her eyes rounded. 'A freak, you mean?'

Joss wasn't having any of that. He wrapped his arm round her and dragged her up against him, where she belonged.

'I'd have gone crazy within weeks, locked up as you were.' It was the truth. He revelled in open spaces and pitting himself against the elements. It was one of the reasons he'd taken to geology. That and the need to prove himself to his father. 'I'd have been a gibbering wreck.'

He lifted his hand to her mouth, tracing the sultry shape of her natural pout, revelling this time in the tiny dart of electricity sparking from that touch.

'You're a survivor, Leila. You should be proud.'

What courage had it taken to survive? To walk away and embrace a new life with a man she didn't know?

Joss wanted to wrap her close and not release her. Assure himself he had her safe where he wanted her—with him. But he forced himself to ease his hold. She'd had coercion enough.

'What now, Leila? What do you want now you're away from all that?'

He waited for her to say she'd take up her studies again or pursue the money Gamil had stolen from her. Obviously she'd want revenge on her stepfather. Who wouldn't?

Yet the tension swarming in his belly had nothing to do with those things. It struck him that, now the truth was out, Leila might demand a release from their marriage.

He wasn't ready to let her go. His whole body stiffened in rejection.

She tilted her head, her sudden smile stealing his breath.

'Since you ask…' she paused and his heart plunged to his toes '…I want to learn to drive.'

CHAPTER TWELVE

'CLUTCH.' THE INSTRUCTION was automatic but unnecessary. Already Leila had her foot on the clutch, changing gears with only a mild grate of the gearbox and a tiny judder of the powerful engine.

Joss watched her tongue slick her bottom lip, her brow crinkle in concentration, and felt an urge to stop the car and pull her into his embrace. To make love to her here despite the bucket seats, gear stick and restricted space in the sports car.

He had it bad when teaching a woman to drive aroused him. Once he'd have scorned the idea of teaching a lover to drive. His connection to the women who passed through his life was fleeting and based solely on pleasure.

Yet this was pleasure too.

Being with Leila, watching her grow in confidence with every turn of the wheel on the deserted estate road. Sharing her excitement at what must be a dazzling taste of freedom after the horrors she'd endured.

Joss wouldn't have missed it for anything.

The idea of another man sharing this moment gouged a hole through his belly. He didn't want to think of her with anyone else. He wanted her with him. Not just for sex, nor her social skills and connections.

He rubbed his chin, puzzling over that.

She'd thanked him profusely when he offered to teach her

on a friend's country estate. As if he bestowed an impossibly precious favour.

He felt a fraud. It was nothing to bring her here. He was the one who basked in the warmth of her radiant smile. Who had the pleasure of watching her excitement and confidence grow. Who'd reap the rewards of that excitement later.

'Sorry.' She grimaced as she changed down for a bend and grated the gearbox again. 'I shouldn't be driving anything so expensive.'

'It's a car, Leila. That's all. It can be repaired or replaced like any other.' His ego had never been caught up in owning status-symbol vehicles. He used four-wheel drives chosen for reliability on his site visits. This top-of-the-range sports model was purely to indulge his love of speed out of the city.

'I suppose I should have waited and organised something more sedate for you.' Had he been selfishly eager to treat her?

Leila shook her head, flyaway strands of mahogany hair catching his shirt as she manoeuvred around a curve and the breeze caught her hair. The scent of it, rich with sunshine and exotic flowers, tingled in his nostrils.

'No! I love it. I love the way it responds to my touch with such power.' Her husky laugh set anticipation bubbling in his bloodstream. Joss thought of the way Leila responded to *his* touch—with eager passion and an innocent generosity that belied the trauma she'd been through.

She was indomitable and resilient.

He'd never known a woman like her.

It struck him that his need to look after her was far removed from the brotherly concern he'd felt for Joanna. Poor Joanna hadn't had the resources to fight the pressures she'd faced. But Leila, despite the panic attacks she seemed to be outgrowing, had an inner strength that shone through. He did no more than give her the chance to be herself.

Her resilience meant she'd be okay when the time came

to part. She didn't *need* him. She wouldn't cling, as so many had before.

Joss frowned, disconcerted that that knowledge brought no satisfaction.

Leila stared up at the canopy of the willow. Sunlight filtered in translucent beams of soft green, giving this shady bower an otherworldly quality. Trailing branches stirred gently in the breeze, brushing the emerald turf. Water chuckled by in a narrow brook at the boundary of their secret picnic spot.

She watched Joss unpacking a hamper and knew he'd chosen this spot especially. Not just for its beauty but because it blended the outdoors with a sense of enclosure—perfect for a woman who until recently had suffered panic attacks leaving the apartment.

Joss's was a practical sympathy—he just got on and *did* things for her without fuss. Wonderful things, like kissing away her anxiety in a lift, even yesterday in an unfamiliar building with strangers present. Her toes curled thinking of that kiss. It felt as if he'd welcomed her *home* when he'd opened his arms and drawn her close.

Afterwards she'd felt dazed and disoriented from what had been only a gentle caress. Yet it had twined ropes of longing round her, binding her to him.

She gulped down a clot of emotion.

'Leila?' Sharp as ever, he noticed. 'Are you okay?'

'How can you ask?' She smiled. Her hands still trembled from the effort of controlling that growling, gorgeously sexy beast of a car. 'I felt like I was flying.'

He shook his head, his one-sided smile plucking at something deep in her chest. 'You weren't going fast enough to get out of fourth gear.'

Leila shrugged. She'd spent so much time behind high walls. Controlling that powerful vehicle, steering it where *she* chose, was stunningly liberating. As was the fact Joss trusted her to manage it.

'But I drove it. I did it myself.'

His smile faded. He nodded, his gaze holding hers so she felt its intensity.

'That you did, Leila.' He turned to the hamper. 'We'd better organise proper lessons so you're not dependent on me finding time to teach you.'

Leila bit back an instant protest. She wanted Joss to teach her. Not because she felt safe with him—that went without saying—but because today had been special, so special she wanted to do it again and again.

The thought stopped her voicing her protest. It was unreasonable to expect him to do this regularly. He ran a multinational corporation! He had back-to-back meetings scheduled for months.

Yet Joss had made it seem natural he should teach her to drive his designer sports car then picnic on a private estate. Just as he made it seem normal they spent so much time together, not just at charity galas and business dinners. They spent quiet evenings reading or watching films and lunched at superb restaurants that somehow stayed off the paparazzi radar.

Leila had got used to being with Joss, relaxing with him, enjoying his company.

Was she too dependent on him?

Surely not. If she'd learned one thing it was independence. She relied on no one but herself.

'What is it?' Joss looked up to see her watching. 'I can't have food on my face—we haven't eaten.'

He drew his hand across his gold-tanned jaw and Leila was sucked into memory. Of her kissing that jaw in the dawn light. Of his bristles teasing her lips. Of the earthy, clean scent of aroused male in her nostrils and the texture of hot silk skin over hard muscles. Pungent pleasure swamped her and desire eddied, a familiar swirl, dragging at her abdomen.

'Nothing.' Why did she have to sound breathless? 'I was just thinking.' Leila blinked and saw his look change from curiosity to heavy-lidded awareness.

Instantly she plunged back into that heady place where nothing mattered except being with Joss. Why did he affect her this way? He'd assured her they'd go their separate ways when they'd sated this need for each other. But it grew stronger, not weaker.

Weeks it had been and she was no closer to pursuing her goals. She hadn't even chosen a course to enrol in. As long as she could remember she'd wanted to be a diplomat, but now the urgency for that career had faded. She drifted, happy to share Joss's life, interested in the snippets he revealed about his business. She'd even wondered about taking a role in managing the land she'd inherited, despite her lack of experience.

Was she in danger of giving up her goals just for the pleasure of being with Joss?

Or had her goals changed? Had her plans been out of loyalty to her father? It struck her that Gamil's disapproval had cemented them because she knew he hated the notion.

What was it she really wanted?

Her heart thudded a tattoo as Joss stood, his eyes on hers as he stretched to his full, imposing height.

His expression told her he'd lost interest in food.

He watched her as if seeking a sign.

Leila drank in the sight of him, solidly muscled and uncompromisingly male. She read desire in those sin-dark eyes and strength in those massive hands. She remembered his tenderness as he kissed her, his generosity as he'd given her free rein with his ruinously expensive car. His teasing as he'd distracted her from fear and supported her growing confidence.

Anticipation welled as Joss strode to her.

He dropped to his knees where she sat, his hand anchoring

her hair from her face. She loved the feel of him massaging her scalp. Pleasure speared every erogenous zone.

'We'll eat later,' he murmured, his mouth a kiss away.

Leila looked into his eyes and her soul shivered at the depth of what she felt. He was…he was…

She couldn't put it into words. Instead she cupped his jaw, felt a tremor of response and pressed her lips to his. Sweet pleasure unfurled.

She'd live for the moment and worry about the future later.

'You'll be fine,' Joss murmured. 'These are your people.'

It wasn't what he said but the way his voice feathered the bare skin of her neck that sent a tide of delight rippling through her.

'And you look stunning.' He touched her wrist, brushing the opal-and-diamond bracelet he'd given her. Between her breasts hung a matching pendant of green opal shot with scarlet fire. It was magnificent, worthy of a queen, and Joss had given it to *her*, saying it reminded him of the fire in her eyes when they argued. And when they made love. He made her feel precious.

Her hand slid down the heavy peacock silk of her designer gown. 'I know what you're doing, Joss. You're trying to distract me.'

Though the Bakhari Embassy in London had been home territory once, a lifetime had passed since then. The imposing mosaic-and-marble reception hall with its crystal chandeliers and glittering throng was a far cry from her memories. She was as nervous as a child playing dress up, summoned to a reception to meet the new sheikh and his bride.

Last time she'd been on Bakhari territory it had been her wedding day. Before that she'd spent years under the tyranny of a man who by Bakhari law had had ultimate power over her. Her love of her homeland was soured by bad memories.

'Am I succeeding?' Joss's mouth curled in a smile that

told her he planned something deliciously wicked for later.
Her heart jolted. In his dinner jacket and bow tie he was the
most potently attractive man she'd ever seen.

'You always succeed.' She let herself fall into the glorious
inky depths of his knowing eyes.

How could she resist? He made her feel life was a secret
to which he alone knew the answer. He offered it to her as
he gathered her close.

The evening passed in a blur. The pleasure of speaking her
native language mixed with bittersweet joy as she renewed
acquaintances severed by years of isolation at Gamil's hands.
He'd stolen her freedom and self-confidence, but also family friends who'd thought she'd chosen to drift away rather
than stay in contact. Meeting people who'd known her parents brought joy leavened with anger.

'Leila.' Joss's voice cut across her thoughts. 'It's our turn.'
They'd made their way to the inner sanctum where the sheikh
and his wife received guests.

Sheikh Zahir of Bakhara was a commanding figure, tall
and broad–shouldered in traditional robes. Only the heavy
gleam of gold on his ring finger and the intricately inlaid
scabbard at his belt relieved the austerity of his garb. That
face—shrewd, proud and determined—didn't need adorn-
ment. He looked as if he'd stepped straight from the desert
into the reception.

His wife, abundantly pregnant and beautiful in dark vio-
let, smiled warmly and nodded at Leila. She placed a hand
on her husband's arm and instantly his features softened as
he inclined his head.

Something sharp jabbed Leila under the ribs. At the sight
of that powerful man so attuned to his wife? Because of the
tenderness in Queen Soraya's eyes as she looked up at her
husband?

It was the impression of an instant yet the powerful connection between them hit Leila with the impact of a force field.

Longing welled up inside her. For what they had. For love, for permanence.

For the things she'd hoped for since she was little and shared the warmth of her parents' love. Since she'd seen beyond her marriage of convenience to the man beneath the drive and hard-nosed business acumen. Joss was tender and patient. He was strong enough not to be threatened by her strength of character. He cared.

What would it be like carrying Joss's child, as Queen Soraya carried the sheikh's? Leila's breath hitched as warmth flooded her. Joss's child…

The sheikh's gaze turned to her. She read curiosity and something that sent anxiety plunging through her.

She grasped Joss's hand and he covered it with his.

Stupid to fear. Her marriage had saved her from Gamil's influence, even if he'd used it to climb the greasy pole of court influence.

She was safe. She was free. Nothing could harm her.

'Joss, it's good to see you.' The sheikh stretched out an arm and Leila watched, perplexed, as they shook hands. Joss knew the sheikh? He'd never mentioned it.

'Your Highness.' Joss drew her forward and introduced her.

To her relief the royal couple were friendly, despite the sheikh's penetrating gaze. Soon they were discussing the recent upgrade of the embassy buildings and plans to renovate the Paris embassy. From there the queen steered discussion to Paris, her favourite city, and Leila found herself sharing reminiscences of the city.

By the time the ambassador called the assembly to quiet, Leila was enjoying herself.

It was only as she surveyed the silent crowd that she saw a familiar face—Gamil.

The blood drained from her face in a rush that chilled to her toes. Her breath hissed between her teeth and she had to work to keep her composure. Why was he in London?

Leila couldn't stop a shudder of hatred and—though she was loath to admit it—fear, at the sight of him.

Joss tightened his grip, his thumb caressing the pulse at her wrist. His gaze was fixed on the far side of the room too. Feeling his strength, Leila realised that whatever came next she could face it.

She wasn't alone any more.

Of the opening speeches Leila heard little. Her head filled with the urgent thrum of blood as her stepfather pushed to a more prominent position. He was opposite, watching the sheikh with an excitement that made her stomach dip in premonition.

There was a pause, a ripple of anticipation across the crowd, and Leila realised the sheikh spoke about the ambassador's retirement and his successor.

Gamil straightened, his hand smoothing his sleeve in a familiar gesture that revealed nervous excitement.

Bile rose in her throat. Gamil had destroyed her mother and tried to destroy her. How could she listen silently to the news he was being elevated to that prestigious position?

The sheikh spoke again and applause thundered. All eyes turned to a distinguished man on the other side of the sheikh: a career diplomat and friend of Leila's father.

Leila clapped the news of his promotion to ambassador but her attention was riveted on Gamil, whose eyes flashed shock and whose jaw worked with suppressed emotion.

'As we are all friends gathered here,' the sheikh continued, 'I'd also like to take this opportunity to acknowledge one of our own.' He gestured across the room at Gamil, addressing him by his full name.

Leila stiffened. What royal honour was he about to bestow? Gamil preened, chest puffed out and smile self-satisfied.

'It's come to my notice that, due to personal family matters—' the sheikh's voice dropped to a steely note '—our advisor Gamil is forced to withdraw from public life.' He paused. 'Permanently.'

Stunned, Leila watched as Gamil opened and shut his mouth as if seeking the nerve to protest the royal announcement. But the Sheikh's grimly carved expression left no doubt this was a royal decree. A decree of exile from the positions Gamil had schemed to make his own.

Gamil turned a sickly colour and Leila realised he'd known nothing of this. He'd expected promotion and instead received the equivalent of banishment.

Her heart pounded as she realised the implications.

Power was Gamil's reason for being and he'd been robbed of it. Publicly. Irrevocably. The sheikh's word was law—there would be no negotiation.

'And on the same subject…' The sheikh gestured to Joss, standing close.

What was happening? Leila looked from one to another, her mind spinning in dazed circles.

'Thank you, Your Highness. Ladies and Gentlemen.' Joss's baritone carried effortlessly.

He paused and flashed a look at Leila. His eyes were bright with something she couldn't name. Something that warmed her to her soul. His fingers threaded hers.

Joss turned back to the reception. 'In view of His Highness's news, and given the widespread interest in my Bakhari enterprise, I have an announcement. As Gamil is retiring to private life, his position on my new company board will be ably taken by his stepdaughter, my wife, Leila Carmody.'

Leila started, eyes widening as Joss turned. She saw satisfaction and a hard, triumphant glitter in his gaze. Applause welled. Dazed, she caught approving looks from familiar faces.

'But I—' She shook her head, trying to take it in. 'I don't have the experience,' she whispered.

'I have faith in you, Leila.' The sincerity in Joss's voice eased the tension clamping her stomach. 'Just one more challenge.' His smile reminded her that he'd been beside her through so many recent challenges.

Would he be beside her now? Surely taking her onto his board wasn't the action of a man planning to say goodbye any time soon. Had he changed his mind about not wanting a permanent relationship?

She barely had time to digest the idea when the sheikh spoke. 'I'm pleased to see another capable woman contributing to our economic future.'

Heat rose in Leila's cheeks. 'Thank you, Your Highness.' She had no idea why he thought her *capable*. She had no business expertise. Then she saw Sheikh Zahir and Joss exchange a look and suddenly so much tumbled into place. This was Joss's doing. Not just the position in his company but what had happened to Gamil.

Her breath stalled in her lungs.

Joss had done that for *her*.

How much had he told the sheikh? She cringed from the idea of anyone else knowing her past, yet turning to find Joss's gaze warm on her, full of tenderness and pride, she knew he'd have shared only what was necessary. And she couldn't regret the outcome.

'Congratulations.' Queen Soraya shook her hand, beaming. 'This means we can pursue our acquaintance. I have an interest in this enterprise too.'

Leila returned her smile, her brain buzzing as excitement fluttered in her stomach. Was she imagining this heralded a new stage in her relationship with Joss?

She was the centre of a congratulatory throng. Old acquaintances and new wished her well. And all the while Joss stood beside her. She was glad of his presence, overcome by what had happened.

She'd wanted to be involved in developing her family's land. Despite the enormous learning curve ahead, this was the opportunity she'd sought. A chance to make her mark. The news was crazy, scary, exhilarating. Yet, she realised, it was exactly what she wanted.

Joss shifted abruptly. She sensed tension in his rangy frame and turned.

Gamil approached, his face mottled with choler, his eyes flat and hard.

'I'll deal with this,' Joss muttered.

'No.' Leila put her hand on his arm, feeling taut muscles flex. 'I will.' She'd face this battle alone.

The rest of the room faded as she paced towards the man who'd made her life hell. The man whose cruelty had turned her world into a prison. She waited for hatred to surface. For that snap and sizzle of defiance. Instead, seeing him defeated and deprived of his grandiose dreams she felt nothing. He was a shadow of the puffed-up figure he'd been.

Leila stopped before him, waiting for his vitriol to spill out, knowing it couldn't harm her. She'd moved on. The knowledge gave her a strength she'd never imagined. She felt ready to take on the world.

Gamil opened his mouth, then, after one burning glare, spun away and barged towards the exit.

Still Leila felt nothing. Till she turned and found Joss watching. The heat of his gaze was a caress of welcome. Of homecoming.

Knowledge slammed into her. Knowledge that had hovered on the edge of her consciousness for weeks.

It was so momentous that the blaze from the chandeliers dipped as the world slid into a blur then back into sharper focus, each detail more vivid than before.

Leila sucked in a stunned breath.

No wonder Gamil had no power over her now.

She had everything she wanted. She had Joss.

CHAPTER THIRTEEN

LEILA STROKED the damp contours of Joss's chest, luxuriating in the aftermath of his loving. He'd barely walked in the door after a morning of meetings before she was in his arms then in his bed.

She stretched, arching her spine as his hand slid down her back then rose to tangle in her hair. She adored the way he touched her—those powerful hands gentle as if she were precious and breakable. Almost as much as she adored the times passion eclipsed gentleness and he took her with fierce urgency, times when it seemed their souls were one.

'We didn't even make it to lunch.' His voice rumbled beneath her as she lay across him.

'Hmm.' She had so much on her mind, food didn't feature.

Excitement stirred as she leaned over to press a kiss to his collarbone. All morning she'd seesawed between delight and trepidation. But after Joss's tender loving she told herself there was no need for nerves. Everything would turn out right. More, it would be *perfect*. She could see herself growing old with this man. Bearing his children.

'What are you smiling about?'

'Can't a woman be happy to see her husband?' She feathered her fingers down his torso and across his ribs to the sensitive spot that always made him shiver. Inevitably he captured her hand.

'How happy?' His voice dropped to a gravelly scratch

that scraped deliciously through her. 'Happy enough to delay lunch a little longer?'

Her smile turned to a knowing grin. 'I could be persuaded.'

Her heart was so full of joy she couldn't keep it to herself any longer. Leila thrust aside the tiny voice of warning that she couldn't quite banish.

She pressed another kiss to his skin, inhaling his salty spice tang. Remembering all he'd done for her, how he *cared*, gave her courage to admit the truth. She didn't want secrets between them.

'I love you, Joss.' Suddenly shy, she didn't meet his eyes, but waited, heart thudding in anticipation.

His chest rose as he took a huge breath. His fingers tightened around hers.

'What brought this on?'

Leila frowned. He didn't sound pleased. His voice had a sharp edge she hadn't heard in ages.

'What do you mean?' Mesmerised, she watched his chest rise again as part of her brain screamed that this wasn't going how she'd hoped. Far from being delighted, Joss sounded suspiciously out of sorts. Had that warning voice been right after all?

Leila shoved the idea aside. She *knew* Joss. He wasn't the cold, emotionally isolated man she'd once thought him. She raised her head. He was staring at the ceiling, brow lined by a ferocious scowl.

Her insides dipped like a swooping roller coaster.

'What led to this announcement?'

He kept his gaze on the ceiling as Leila surveyed his taut features. His mouth was flat, pulled tight. His nose was pinched and lines carved deep around his mouth, giving him an uncompromising air.

Joy turned to wariness. Where was the man who seconds ago had burned hot with desire, who'd held her against his heart? He *was* real. She hadn't imagined the changes in Joss since their marriage. They'd been profound. Enough to make her risk revealing her own fragile hopes.

'I realised how I felt about you.' Too late to rescind the words. She was committed now.

'When?' Still he stared unblinkingly at the ceiling. Leila was tempted to wave her hand over his face to grab his attention. Yet the taut flex of his muscles beneath her, his whole body stiffening, told her he was totally focused. 'Last night, when I gave you a seat on the board?'

Leila frowned. He sounded…almost sarcastic.

'Over a period of time.' Not for the life of her would she admit he was right. The knowledge had struck like a lightning bolt as she'd met his eyes and felt that overwhelming sense of belonging, just after he and Sheikh Zahir had broken their news.

'You don't have to do this.' His mouth twisted. 'I don't expect more from you.'

'Do what?' She shook her head, her hair sliding around them both. She watched it slip across his broad shoulder.

'Pretend to feel more. I know you're grateful about Gamil but it's unnecessary.'

'Grateful.' The word sank like a stone in still water. 'You think I'm grateful?'

'Aren't you?' Finally he turned, skewering her with a glittering stare that should have sizzled her blood. Instead she felt hoarfrost crackle across her skin.

This had been the happiest day of her life and suddenly, inexplicably, it was going completely awry. She knew of his emotional scars but had told herself they'd begun to heal. Surely a man as caring and generous as Joss deserved love.

Had she fooled herself into thinking he was ready for that?

Fear engulfed her.

Joss looked into smoky green eyes and felt a pang of loss so keenly it stole his breath.

Everything had been so good—too good, he realised now. He should have known it wouldn't last.

Hadn't he had moments of premonition these past months? Moments of pleasure so exquisite he knew they must be fleeting? Because they were all tied up with Leila.

Because happiness that centred on another person was a mistake.

Because everyone left eventually. Or betrayed. Or used you till they'd eaten you up like acid eating skin, scouring till there was nothing left to feel.

He turned away from her intent gaze, back to the ceiling. Smooth, white, perfectly blank, it should have soothed.

His gut twisted in a searing knot that sent bile up to burn his throat.

Nothing soothed. Not now.

It was too late.

He'd let himself pretend this wasn't dangerous. That they could go on as they were.

He should have known better.

I love you, Joss.

Even now he felt a desperate urge to cling to Leila's words. To forget all he'd learned about love and loss and take a chance on the mirage being real this time.

He swiped his hand across his face.

Hell! He hadn't wanted to believe so badly since he was ten. Since Joanna had run away and left him, despite her supposed love for him. Since he'd failed her and proved himself unworthy.

I love you, Joss. How often had his mother said that? Used the words to tie her children to her, only to reject them whenever they behaved like normal kids rather than extensions of her ego?

I love you, Joss. How many times had some woman simpered those words, clutching tight, hoping for more of the material riches he could give?

I love you, Joss.

They were a death knell to the happiness he and Leila had shared.

He gulped swirling nausea, skin crawling at the notion she might have deliberately set out to ensnare him with that supposedly magic formula.

Yet even worse was the suspicion Leila meant it. That she'd become emotionally invested in an illusion. That she believed him capable of returning...love.

Joss put a hand to her shoulder and moved her aside as he jackknifed to sit on the edge of the bed. He gulped huge draughts of air yet couldn't fill his lungs. His ears buzzed and he thought he was going to black out. He leaned forward, elbows on knees, trying to calm the writhing knot of pain where his belly and his heart had been.

'Joss. Say something!'

His mouth twisted. What was there to say?

Her hand closed on his shoulder, clutching. As if she knew she'd lost him?

Damn it. He wasn't ready for this to end. Not yet. Selfishly he wanted the pleasure to last. Pleasure with no complications.

He surged from the bed and stood facing the windows.

'We said no strings. Remember?' His voice wasn't his own, rasping like flint on stone.

'Things have changed.' She sounded bewildered. Joss raked his hand through his hair, telling himself it wasn't real. It couldn't be love. He didn't inspire such affection. She offered what she thought he wanted to hear.

'You don't owe me. Last night—' He hand slashed the air. 'Last night was about setting things right, that's all. You don't need to feel...obligated.'

For long seconds she said nothing.

'I'm grateful for what you did with Gamil,' she said finally. 'But that's not why I love you.'

Her words taunted him. Words he'd once craved but finally

learnt to despise. They dragged through his dark soul, dredging the depths as if seeking the needy boy he'd once been.

Joss swung to face her, blocking out the emotion that rose unbidden at those lethal words. He wasn't a naive kid any more. He wasn't vulnerable.

'*Don't*…say that. I told you it's not necessary.' The more she said it, the further they slipped into a no-win situation.

She clutched the sheet to her breasts and he knew it was too late. The damage was done. There was no going back. Inside him a raw howl of loss rose, a wordless tearing roar of rage at her naivety in ending what they'd had. It had been glorious, spectacular. Addictive.

He read her hurt and knew she'd never forgive him for what he had to do.

Even so, he wanted selfishly to buy more time. He wasn't ready to release her. He had to try to make her see.

'It's okay, Leila. I know you didn't mean it.' Joss spread his hands wide.

Leila stared at the man she loved, wondering at the change in him. His face was grim and pale beneath his tan and he refused to meet her gaze.

Why wouldn't he look at her?

Why this farce that she didn't know her own mind?

'I do mean it.' The words spilled out, and she recognised his expression now—anger. So fierce it shrivelled the tender bud of joy she'd nursed all morning.

It was like watching Dr Jekyll transform into Mr Hyde, seeing Joss's expression shut down into stark lines of disapproval.

'Don't, Leila.' Was that desperation in his voice? Leila leaned forward, looking for signs of the man who'd made love to her passionately such a short time ago. 'You'll regret it later.'

She sat straighter. She regretted it now. She'd been so sure of Joss's feelings. But far from reciprocating what she felt, he acted as if she'd done something terrible.

'We'll go on as before,' he said, pacing the floor. His nakedness only reinforced his aura of formidable strength. 'We can forget about this.' He waved his hand dismissively as if her announcement was a mere nothing.

Through her confusion anger drilled down.

'I don't want to forget it.' Couldn't he see how vital this was to both of them? Couldn't he *feel* it?

Joss swung round, his gaze pinioning her with a force that sucked the air from her lungs. He looked…savage. Desperate. Furious.

'It's the only way.'

Leila wrapped the sheet tighter. Despite the room's temperature control she was chilled to the marrow. 'What do you mean?'

He'd stopped pacing and stood, arms akimbo and jaw thrust forward, the image of male aggression. 'We had an understanding, remember?'

'If you mean the no-sex rule, I didn't see you complaining about breaking that.' Indignation bubbled inside her.

'Of course not. That was mutually agreed. I'm talking about no strings attached. No emotional entanglement.' He wrapped his palm around the back of his neck and for a moment looked like a man out of his depth, wrestling with forces beyond his control.

Before her sympathy could stir, he went on. 'You're breaking our agreement.'

Agreement? Joss was concerned about an *agreement*?

What about the fact she'd fallen in love with him? That she'd bared her feelings and been rejected? Had he any concept of how much she hurt right now?

'You don't love me?' Her voice was brittle, barely penetrating the thickened atmosphere clogging the room.

But he heard. She could tell by the way he stiffened.

'I don't do love. I made that clear in the beginning.'

Pain scythed through her and she wrapped one arm across her belly as if to ward off a physical blow. She hunched forward, her breath coming in short, hard gasps. He sounded cold as ice. Not the warm, generous, caring man she'd fallen for.

Had he been a mirage?

She'd heard his pain when he spoke of his family and the need to be alone. But everything he'd done, the tenderness he'd shown, had convinced her to hope.

'We had an agreement.' He stood before her, arms folded. 'I give you money and you act as my hostess. Beyond that— sex for mutual pleasure, that's all.' His gaze bore into her. 'I'm willing to overlook this morning and continue as we were.'

Leila couldn't believe what she was hearing. She swung her legs off the bed but didn't stand. She had a horrible feeling her legs wouldn't support her.

'You're happy for us to live together, and have sex of course—' her voice dripped disdain '—as long as there aren't messy emotions like love.' Her voice quivered on the last word, echoing the shuddering pain in her heart.

He raised his eyebrows. 'Don't look surprised. That's what we agreed.' He paced closer, his expression grim. 'We do this my way, take it or leave it. That's the deal—it always has been.'

Leila gasped. Revulsion swirled through her.

Deal! He had the temerity to talk of deals after what they'd shared?

Looking up at Joss's adamant face, his ferocious scowl and narrowed eyes, she was reminded suddenly of Gamil. Of how he'd demanded and ordered—always imposing his will, never considering anyone else.

Could she have been so wrong about Joss? Right now he was every bit as domineering and unreasonable as her stepfather—the epitome of everything she'd learned to loathe.

She couldn't believe it. Yet surely now, if ever, was the time for him to show his true colours.

Had she let love blind her to his selfishness? Had passion skewed her judgement so badly? She was inexperienced about men and lust—had she confused the situation?

No! Surely not.

Desperately she sought some sign of the Joss she knew in the steely-eyed man before her. Just a hint of softening.

Disappointment crushed her as he stared back, showing no tenderness or understanding. One thing was clear. There was no softness in him, only selfish demands and disapproval.

He didn't love her.

Suddenly Leila felt aged beyond her years. Even breathing took more effort than she could manage. Was this how her mother had felt when she realised Gamil had duped her? When she realised he didn't truly love her? That he didn't have the capacity to care for anyone but himself?

Everything in Leila revolted at the idea. Not Joss! But the man before her stood solid and accusing.

Shakily Leila got to her feet, hauling the sheet up.

'You don't want a wife.' She drew an uneven breath. 'You want a woman who'll share her body and ask for nothing but money.' Bile rose. 'You want a whore.'

Joss's head jerked back as if she'd slapped him but he didn't move. 'I told you at the beginning, Leila. I never wanted a real wife. No emotions, no kids, no complications.'

Leila swayed as the cold, hard clarity of his words struck deeply in her wounded heart.

How had she ever imagined he'd cared? It had been convenient for him to help her overcome her fear of going out. It made her a more useful companion. Perhaps he'd even banked on gratitude making her more amenable to sex. She swallowed convulsively.

As for what he'd done to Gamil, maybe it wasn't about her

after all. Maybe it was easier having an inexperienced, compliant wife on the board than her wily stepfather.

No man who truly cared would treat her this way.

Leila's head swam as she tried and failed to make sense of this nightmare.

One thing remained constant—the arrogance carved on Joss's face as he waited for her response.

'No emotions, no kids, no complications.' She repeated his words in a scratchy whisper. Her lips curved in a grim smile that held no humour. 'Too bad, Joss. It's too late.'

'Just because you said—'

Leila lifted an imperious hand. 'Forget that.' She shied from going there. The pain was too raw. 'There are other complications.' She drew a slow breath, wondering how this morning's incandescent joy had turned sour so quickly. 'I found out this morning—we're expecting a baby.'

The last of the colour drained from Joss's face, leaving it sickly pale. He staggered back, grabbing at the wall as if needing support.

'You're lying.' His whisper was hoarse with shock and, could it be—revulsion?

If she'd needed anything to convince her she'd deceived herself, seeing stark horror on Joss's face did it. Her skin prickled and drew tight.

She slipped a hand protectively across her stomach.

'I don't lie, Joss.'

How she found her voice she didn't know. Her body kept functioning even when he'd dealt her heart a lethal blow.

He opened his mouth as if to speak but no sound emerged. The pulse at his temple pounded out of control and the tendons in his neck and shoulders stood out rigidly.

Leila waited. Waited because even now she couldn't believe it could end like this. She waited for Joss to haul her into his arms and apologise. To say he loved her. That he was ecstatic at her news.

She'd wait a lifetime, she realised finally. Because she'd been mistaken in him. She'd taken casual generosity for real caring. Sex for true passion and love.

'Don't bother asking,' she said through gritted teeth, despising herself for even now wanting more. 'Mother and baby are both healthy.'

With one final sweeping glance at the man who'd taken her heart and ripped it apart, she stalked out the door.

When Leila emerged from her room hours later, it was to the news Joss had packed his bags and left. Urgent negotiations overseas, the housekeeper said.

'When is he due back?' Leila didn't know whether to be relieved she didn't need to face him or furious he'd gone. They had things to sort out.

Her blood sizzled in renewed fury that almost eclipsed the hurt gouging at her heart.

'I'm sorry, madam.' Mrs Draycott's gaze skittered away. 'I had the impression… That is, I…' She wiped her hands down her skirt. 'I believe he'll be gone quite some time. He didn't talk about returning.'

Leila read the woman's discomfort and a chill descended that froze her to the spot.

Even after hours of digesting today's scene, she hadn't quite been able to believe it was the end of all she'd held so dear. Belief in the man she loved. Her dream that they'd build a life together, raise and love the child they'd created between them.

She understood some of Joss's reaction had been the product of shock. She'd convinced herself that when he thought things through he wouldn't be so adamant. Whatever his hang-ups about family, he couldn't throw away what they had.

It seemed he could.

He'd left without a backward glance. Without a murmur of regret or apology.

Leila told herself she didn't care. She and her child were better off alone than with a man like that. Yet it took a superhuman effort to ignore the shudder of pain that hit her and walk carefully back to her room.

She had plans to make.

CHAPTER FOURTEEN

JOSS SWITCHED OFF the engine and stared at the house across the quiet street. Rambling, set back from the road in its own garden, it looked solid and comfortable.

Perhaps it was the sunlight glinting off the large windows or the mellow warmth of old brick that gave the illusion. Perhaps the ornamented chimneys or budding roses around the door. No matter how illogical that bricks and mortar should convey anything so sentimental, the place looked like *home*. A warm, welcoming home such as he'd never known. The sort of home he could imagine Leila living in. Leila and their child.

He caught his breath as white-hot pain seared his chest.

He had no right to be here. He'd given up that right when he'd turned his back on Leila and what she thought was her love for him.

The pain twisted hard and sharp, skewering his sternum.

He grimaced, telling himself he wasn't surprised Leila had opted for comfort rather than a trendy apartment. He recalled her gardening magazines and how she'd reminisced about her childhood, the importance of a home.

This would be a real home. Not because it was charming and reassuringly solid, but because Leila would make it so. Leila with her warmth and determination and optimism.

What right had he to barge in? It was her sanctuary. She deserved it after what she'd been through.

What right had he, who knew nothing of homes or love, to intrude?

Joss looked again. This time the roses around the door and either side of the gate looked like thorned sentinels, keeping out unwanted visitors. The very warmth of the old house was a reminder of why he had no place here. He'd only brought her misery.

He reached for the thick wad of papers on the passenger seat, the envelope crackling in his grasp. Opening the door and striding across that road was the hardest thing he'd ever done.

Leila hummed as she knelt over the garden bed, weeding. That was why she didn't hear anything. The first hint she wasn't alone was when a shadow blocked the sun and she looked up to see feet coming to a stop on the gravel path. Large feet wearing hand-stitched loafers.

Emotion trembled through her. An instantaneous recognition she fought to douse.

It wasn't him. It would never be him. Hadn't she learned that after two months' silence? She'd left Joss's apartment, left his life, and heard not a word from him.

Nevertheless it took Leila a moment to harness her wayward emotions and don a calm expression.

'Can I help you?' She looked up, past long, long legs covered in washed denim, over a flat male belly, past a casual jacket and white shirt to wide, straight shoulders and a jaw honed from steel.

Her heart gave a great leap and lodged somewhere near her throat. She thrust out a hand to keep her balance as she swayed backwards.

'Leila!' He lunged towards her then froze as if recalling he had no right to touch her.

Her eyes widened as she took him in. He was as spectacular as ever—more so; the casual clothes suited him, as did the curl of dark hair brushing his collar. In the clear spring sunshine he looked like everything she'd secretly dreamed of for so long.

The realisation stiffened her sinews and finally engaged her brain. Jerkily she got to her feet, backing from the path till she realised she was retreating and planted her feet.

'Are you all right?'

Leila teetered on the brink of believing that was concern in his voice. But she'd learned better.

His gaze swept her. Did she imagine it lingered on her belly? She stifled the urge to slip her hand protectively over her baby.

'Joss.' Her tone was flat. 'What are you doing here?'

He swallowed hard, his mouth firming, as if he didn't like being challenged.

Leila took off her soil-encrusted gloves and dropped them at her feet. Bad enough to be caught on her knees, but did he have to find her in gardening clothes?

She'd wanted, if she ever saw him again, to look cool and sophisticated, calmly unimpressed by his presence. Yet heat rose in her cheeks at his scrutiny and her breath came in uneven little pants. Valiantly she strove to calm herself. He'd be gone soon. He wouldn't linger.

'You're looking well.'

She opened her mouth to respond then closed her lips. She refused to bandy polite greetings. Though now she looked more closely he appeared tired, the hollows around his eyes and in his lean cheeks more pronounced. Obviously devoting himself to his business empire was demanding.

When she said nothing his eyes narrowed as if trying to read her thoughts.

'Aren't you going to invite me in?' He gestured to the house behind her. She'd bought it with the funds she'd earned by signing his precious agreement and marrying him. That house was her sanctuary and her hope for the future.

'No!' Her vehemence surprised him. She saw it in his raised eyebrows. But she didn't want him on her territory. It would be harder than ever to eradicate memories of Joss once she'd let him into her house. 'That's not necessary. We can talk here.' She folded her arms.

On tenterhooks she watched him breathe deeply, his nostrils flaring. Would he try to force her hand?

'How are you, Leila?'

It was the last thing she'd expected. What was more, his voice held that soft gravel note she'd learnt to heed because it signalled deep emotion.

Her fingers dug into her arms through her shirt. Who was she kidding? She'd thought she'd known Joss but she'd been wrong. So wrong it would be laughable if it weren't tragic.

'I'm well.' She didn't ask how he was. She told herself it was because she didn't care but she feared it was because she cared too much. She didn't trust him, didn't like him, but remnants of her feelings for him still lingered.

That was why she had to get rid of him.

'And the baby?' His voice dropped, rolling right through her belly to where their child nestled. This time she couldn't prevent her instinctive gesture, palm to abdomen, as if to shield it from danger.

Anger surged within her. At him for having the gall to ask. At herself because she'd longed for him to acknowledge their child, though she knew it was pointless.

She opened her mouth to sneer that it was none of his business, but stopped.

'The baby is fine.' She dragged in a sharp breath as pain, jagged and raw, sliced through her. Then words she hadn't been aware of forming spilled out. 'Were you hoping it was all a mistake? Or that maybe I'd miscarried and you wouldn't have to worry about *complications*? Is that it?'

Once before she'd seen shock pare his features to the bone and colour ebb from his face. She saw it again now and it cut her to the quick. There was no mistaking his reaction as anything but genuine.

Shame surfaced. What had she come to that she was so vitriolic?

'I'm sorry,' she whispered, appalled. The surge of emotion ebbed abruptly, leaving her feeling wobbly. Her shoulders sagged; the weariness she'd fought for weeks dragged at her so suddenly she felt light-headed.

'Leila?' This time when the world tilted he didn't pull back. His hand was hot through her sleeve, his touch firm and sustaining. 'You need to sit.'

Eyes the colour of twilight locked with hers and she felt something shift in her chest. Leila squeezed her eyes shut, trying to keep it out, but already she felt warmth flowing through her. From his touch, his concern.

What a fool! There was nothing between them, there never had been. Yet still she longed...

'This way.' His tone and his touch were gentle enough to soothe her shredded nerves. She opened her eyes and let him lead her to a garden seat.

'I'm sorry.' Her voice stretched thin as she lowered herself to the seat. She felt like an old, old woman, weary beyond her years. 'That was uncalled for.' She blinked hot eyes and brushed at a smear of soil on her loose shirt.

'I deserved it.'

Leila's head jerked up and she met his gaze as he stood before her. Had she heard right?

'But believe me,' he continued, 'I want nothing more than for you and the baby to thrive. I want only good for you both.'

Staring up at him, she almost believed he cared, *really* cared. Except he'd left her in no doubt that was impossible. Her heart cracked.

'Why are you here, Joss?'

He took a breath as if about to say something momentous.

Yet no words came. His eyes held a shuttered look she hadn't a hope of reading. At his side one big hand curled into a fist.

If she didn't know better she'd think him nervous.

'Because of that?' She gestured to the large envelope in his other hand. She hadn't wanted to acknowledge it, guessing it contained divorce documents.

She wished she could be blasé about ending what was simply a legal contract. But she wasn't her parents' daughter for nothing. She believed in love and family. She craved them. She craved Joss, with a silent fervour that defied logic.

Except the Joss she craved was a figment of her imagination, a man she'd invented based on a little kindness and a whole lot of sexual magnetism.

He wasn't real.

That knowledge gave her the strength to reach out for the envelope he crushed in his fist.

'Is this for me?' Finally he opened his hand. Her pulse skipped as she took the envelope and ice slithered down her spine despite the sunshine. She suppressed a silent keening wail. This was so far from what she'd dreamed.

But she'd deal with it. She'd be strong and face this as she faced everything else.

'You want me to send it back when I've signed it?' Leila was proud of her even tone.

Joss blinked, his brow furrowing. 'They're for you. Reading material for the board meeting that's coming up.'

Board meeting? Joss had come to give her agenda papers for a meeting? She sagged back in her seat, her heart thrumming out of rhythm.

Nothing about this meeting made sense, least of all Joss, who stood looking as poleaxed as she felt.

'Joss?' She tried to collect herself. 'Why are you here? Your staff could have sent the papers.'

His eyes burned into hers. She felt the impact right to her

toes curling tight in her gardening boots. He only had to look at her and she wanted to believe—

'I had to see you. I needed to make sure you were all right.' His voice was a harsh riptide of sound that undercut her determination.

'Why? You don't want complications, remember?' Weariness rather than bitterness laced her words. She'd been bitter so long. Now, looking at his taut features, she felt regret and pain. And that welling of emotion she hadn't been able to crush.

She looked away. She needed to be alone. Needed never to see him again. Maybe then she'd convince herself this would work out for the best.

Leila blinked as he dropped to his knees before her. Large hands gathered hers.

She tried to pull back but his hold was firm. And—dreadful to admit—part of her revelled in his touch.

This would be the last time he held her.

'Because you were hurting so much. Because when I finally got past my posturing and my fear, I realised how cruel I'd been.'

Fear? Joss didn't do fear. Just as he didn't do emotional entanglements.

'I told you, I'm okay.' Yet she couldn't gather the strength to tug her hands free. She bit her lip, hating her weakness.

Slowly he shook his head. 'No, you're not. And that's my fault.' He nodded at the envelope on the seat beside her. 'The papers were an excuse. I needed to see you and apologise.' He drew in a ragged breath. 'I was a louse, a complete bastard. I deserve for you to hate me but I had to see if there was anything I could do, to make things easier.'

'Easier?' Her voice was scratchy as she strove to process his words.

His hold tightened. 'You…cared for me, Leila. I threw that in your face.' He shook his head. 'I shouldn't have taken out my fears on you. I know I can't fix things but I wanted to apologise and—'

'What fears? I don't understand.' Joss was powerful and determined, the strongest individual she knew. She'd leaned on his strength time and again. 'Joss?'

His mouth tugged up at one side in what might pass for a smile if she hadn't see the agony in his eyes. Leila's heart pounded hard in sympathy, even as she told herself she shouldn't get dragged in. She was well rid of the man who'd hurt her so devastatingly.

'I was scared, Leila, petrified.' His voice was low and she had to lean forward to catch it. 'I still *am*. That's why I turned on you.'

'Don't talk in riddles.' She tried to tug her hands free, wondering if this was some convoluted scheme to dupe her. But why?

Joss released one of her hands but planted the other over his chest, pressed to his heart. Heat spread from the point of contact. His heart beat to the same frantic rhythm as hers.

It didn't mean anything. Yet the look in his eyes dragged at her resistance.

'I told you I don't do emotions. I *can't* do emotions.'

Leila opened her mouth to disagree but his ravaged expression stopped her.

'I've never had love.' He wasn't looking at her now, but over her shoulder, into the distance. 'That's no excuse, just an explanation. Every time someone told me they loved me, I got hurt, till I steeled myself never to be hurt again. My parents claimed to love me but they only cared about their egos. Love was a blackmail weapon, using us to play their sordid games to best each other. All my life, whenever someone claimed to love me it was about what they could get. Even my sister—' He sucked in a deep breath. 'I loved her but I couldn't protect her and when she left I knew she hadn't cared enough about me to stay.'

Leila's hand moved convulsively against him and he grimaced.

'I know. I was as selfish as my parents, believing that. I was a kid and didn't know better. But deep down I *did* know I wasn't cut out for love. I don't inspire deep feelings in anyone. And as the years went by I realised I wasn't able to love anyone either. I lacked the capacity.'

'Joss, that's absurd.' She'd known he'd been damaged by his past, but to believe he wasn't capable of love!

His eyes cut to her and the force of what she read there dried her protests.

'It's true. I got accustomed to using people and being used—life was a series of barters. Sex for a few trinkets and some good times. The closest I came to love as an adult was when a woman claimed to love me in the hope I'd set her up financially.'

'That's horrible!' It was no more than she'd expected, but hearing it put so brutally was shocking.

He shrugged. 'It's what I expected. Until you.'

Joss stroked his thumb over the back of her hand where it rested on his chest. She told herself she should yank her hand away but there was a disconnect between thought and action. She couldn't do it.

'With you I felt…things I'd never experienced. When you said you loved me I desperately wanted it to be true. But I didn't dare believe it.' He shook his head. 'It was easier to believe you were mistaken or lying than that you loved me.'

'Oh, Joss.' Leila's heart rolled over as she read his pain. Guilt struck her. She should have tried harder to convince him, not given up so easily.

'I'm not after sympathy. I just need to explain why I turned on you and apologise.'

'You already have.'

He looked surprised. 'It's not enough.'

'No, it's not.' Mixed with her sympathy was anger. Anger

that a man so intelligent should have put them through all this because he couldn't comprehend anything as straightforward and wonderfully simple as love. 'You talk as if there's a wall around you, cutting you off from love. All you have to do is reach out and trust your feelings.'

He hesitated. 'I see now that it's possible—in theory.'

At her puzzled look he continued, 'After you left—' his voice dipped '—I couldn't work. I couldn't function. Nothing held my attention. I wanted...' He shook his head. 'I couldn't have what I wanted so I found something else to occupy my time. I traced my sister Joanna's movements. I thought finding her grave might help put the past behind me.'

Leila wanted to ask what it was he wanted, but he continued.

'Eventually I found her.' Emotion flickered in his gaze. 'She hadn't died at fifteen as I'd been told, she just disappeared.'

At Leila's gasp he nodded. 'I guess I was told she died to keep me quiet. I was asking about her all the time.' He rubbed his jaw with his free hand. 'So for weeks I've had investigators searching.'

'You found her?' Leila's heart was in her mouth.

'I did.' The quiet satisfaction in his smile was balm to her shredded nerves. 'She's alive and living in the wilds of Yorkshire with her farmer husband and three kids.'

'And she'd never thought to contact you?' Anger stirred within her at the thought of all those wasted years when Joss had had no one.

His smile died. 'Apparently she tried once, a few years after she left. She was living on the streets and our mother told her she couldn't come back into our lives until she'd cleaned up her act. Joanna was told as far as I was concerned she was dead and it was better that way.'

'That's appalling.' Leila reached out and stroked his hair

from his forehead, needing the connection, needing to comfort him.

'I warned you—my mother *was* appalling.' He captured her hand in his and she welcomed his touch—so familiar. 'But she's gone and Joanna—she's happier than I ever remember. And she's living proof that I was wrong. That our family *can* find love.'

His eyes glittered fiercely and she could have sworn heat arced between them.

'You thought it was a family curse?' Leila was breathless.

'I thought it likely, given my experiences.'

'Joss Carmody, for an intelligent man, sometimes you can be totally stupid!'

He nodded and tugged her closer so she leaned forwards in her seat. 'I know. I've been a fool in all sorts of ways. Worse, I've been a coward. I wanted your love but I was too scared I'd get hurt.'

Leila's heart jumped and her airways jammed at the expression in his eyes. A flicker of excitement stirred.

'What are you saying, Joss?'

'I…fell in love with you, Leila.' His hands tightened and she revelled in his touch. 'I know it's too late, that I've destroyed what you felt, but I had to let you know. And tell you I'm here whenever you need me. Whenever either of you need me. You or the baby.'

The world stood still around them. Even the clouds stopped moving and the drone of a distant car faded as she read the emotion blazing in his face. Hope rose, a trembling, fragile bud.

Did she have the courage to reach out and grasp it?

Could it be true? She wanted to believe it with every atom of her being.

'When did you fall in love, Joss?'

'I don't know. It was a bit at a time. When you kissed me

in the lift that first time and I thought I'd died and gone to heaven.'

Heat crept up her throat as she remembered the no-holds-barred passion of that kiss.

'When you stood up to me, whenever I tried to get my own way without compromise. When I learned how brave you'd been with Gamil.'

Leila shook her head. 'I wasn't brave. I—' His index finger on her lips stopped her words. She tasted salt and Joss and had to fight the instinct to suck his finger into her mouth and taste him better. Hunger slammed into her. It thrilled and appalled her.

'When you drove my Ferrari that first time and managed not to crash it.'

'You're such a *man*!'

His broad shoulders lifted in a shrug and his smile made her heart flip over. 'So sue me.'

Then his grin faded. 'You deserve to know, Leila. I had to apologise and tell you how I felt.'

She looked into his stern face and felt again that throb of impatience.

'And that's all?'

He looked genuinely perplexed.

Slowly her anger faded. It struck her anew that he really was completely inexperienced when it came to love.

It was up to her to educate him.

Leila surged to her feet and paced away.

'Much as I enjoy having you on your knees apologising, I prefer a man who stands up for himself.'

An instant later he stood before her, potently masculine, puzzled and ever so slightly challenging.

'I want a man who believes me when I say I'm in love and doesn't think that will change just because of harsh words or a misunderstanding, no matter how severe.' She raised her brows. 'I want a man who understands when I love it's not negotiable, not put aside easily or lightly.'

'I see.' His deep voice curled tight around her and she shivered.

'I need a man whose love is like that too. Not a fair-weather lover who's only around in the good times.'

'Someone who's there through thick and thin.' Joss nodded and took a pace closer, blocking her exit.

'Precisely.' She swallowed, noting a gleam in his eyes that hadn't been there before. 'I want a man who will be with me and my child for ever.'

Her words hung between them, like a fragile ribbon extended over a yawning void.

'It's a big ask.' His voice was sombre, his face stern.

She lifted her chin. 'My child deserves a father who will love her and support her always.'

'Her?' Joss stepped closer, the heat of his body encompassing her.

'Or him.'

'Or both,' he whispered, trailing his fingertips across her jaw and down her throat, till her senses rioted and her hormones surged. She shivered under his caress.

'Oh,' she breathed. The heat in Joss's eyes needed no interpretation. Leila felt a shimmy of answering arousal deep in her womb.

He lowered his head towards her, but stopped a kiss away, eyes locked with hers. Hope, fear and profound excitement melded within her.

'Leila Carmody, can you forgive me for being such a fool and hurting you so badly?'

'I can.' She watched his eyes squeeze shut for a moment on a sigh of relief and knew she'd been right after all. The man she'd fallen for was no mirage.

'Will you consider staying as my wife, the love of my life, always?'

Words failed as emotion swamped her.

'Could you trust me to love and honour you and be true to you always? Could you help me try to be a good father, the sort of father I always wanted?'

She reached out and squeezed his arm. 'You'll be a wonderful father.' The thought of his patience, his tenderness and encouragement, made her heart swell.

'Does that mean you will?' Joss's voice was unsteady. His hesitancy cut her to the core.

'I think I could.' Her heart pounded a rough tattoo.

'You think?' One dark eyebrow rose.

'I could be persuaded.'

'Could you indeed?' In one swift move he swept her up into his embrace. 'I've a good mind not to let you go until you say yes.' Leila wanted to stay there for ever in his arms. This close she read his fierce possessiveness.

'So much for humility.'

His grin tugged at her heartstrings.

'It didn't suit me. Anyway, I thought you wanted a man who'd stand up for himself.'

Leila smiled, relieved to see her own Joss back.

'Seriously, Leila. You're sure? This isn't just about the baby? I'll be there for our child whether we're together or not.'

Leila punched him lightly on the arm, her heart singing as she realised he took this every bit as seriously as she did. 'I'm absolutely sure, Mr Carmody. We come as a package deal, take it or leave it.'

'Oh, I'll take it, Mrs Carmody. Believe me, I'll take it.'

His kiss was swift and possessive and over too soon. But Leila didn't complain because he strode up the steps to the house and shouldered open the front door.

They had come home.

* * * * *

the CRITTER club

Liz's Pie in the Sky

by Callie Barkley ❤ illustrated by Tracy Bishop

LITTLE SIMON

New York London Toronto Sydney New Delhi

LITTLE SIMON

An imprint of Simon & Schuster Children's Publishing Division · 1230 Avenue of the Americas, New York, New York 10020 · First Little Simon paperback edition October 2021. Copyright © 2021 by Simon & Schuster, Inc. All rights reserved, including the right of reproduction in whole or in part in any form.

LITTLE SIMON is a registered trademark of Simon & Schuster, Inc., and associated colophon is a trademark of Simon & Schuster, Inc. For information about special discounts for bulk purchases, please contact Simon & Schuster Special Sales at 1-866-506-1949 or business@simonandschuster.com.

The Simon & Schuster Speakers Bureau can bring authors to your live event. For more information or to book an event contact the Simon & Schuster Speakers Bureau at 1-866-248-3049 or visit our website at www.simonspeakers.com.

Designed by Brittany Fetcho.

Manufactured in the United States of America 0821 MTN 10 9 8 7 6 5 4 3 2 1

Cataloging-in-Publication Data is available for this title from the Library of Congress.

ISBN 978-1-5344-8712-3 (hc)

ISBN 978-1-5344-8711-6 (pbk)

ISBN 978-1-5344-8713-0 (ebook)

Table of Contents

Recipe for Fun

Liz Jenkins was the first to the lunch table. She sat down closest to the cafeteria windows. Outside, there was a large maple tree. Each day, more of its leaves were golden yellow. Liz smiled. Fall was her favorite time of year.

Liz's friends Marion and Amy sat down next.

"That spelling test was hard," said Amy. "Wasn't it?"

It was Friday. Like every Friday, their teacher, Mrs. Sienna, had quizzed them on their spelling words right before lunch.

"Lots of those words had silent letters," Marion replied as she unwrapped her bagel. "But I think I got them all."

Liz nodded. That sounded about right. Marion almost always got 100 percent on spelling tests.

Ellie was last to the lunch table.

"Did anybody know the bonus word?" Ellie asked them with a frown. "Cornucopia?"

"I did!" Liz replied. "That's a horn-shaped basket thing. We always put one on our Thanksgiving buffet."

Liz was the artsy one in her house. So she was always in charge of decorating for Thanksgiving. She filled the cornucopia with small pumpkins and gourds in wacky shapes. Plus some red and green apples for color.

Liz sighed. She gazed out again at the golden maple tree. She loved everything about fall. The leaves. The weather.

And *especially* trips to Marigold Lake!

Liz's family had a cabin there. And that very weekend, Liz's friends were coming up to stay!

Before long, the spelling test was old news. The girls were excited about their autumn getaway.

"Remember the last time we were all there?" Liz asked her friends. "Roasting marshmallows over the campfire?"

Ellie giggled. "Remember that stick I thought was a snake?"

"And how I flipped the canoe?" Amy said, blushing a little bit.

"And the baby mice?" Marion added.

"Awwwww," all the girls said together. They had found several teeny, tiny baby mice in the cabin. But there had been no mama mouse in sight.

Luckily for the mice, the girls had a safe place to take them. It was their very own animal rescue shelter, The Critter Club. The four of them ran the shelter with the help of Amy's mom, a veterinarian. Dr. Purvis helped the girls care for the baby mice until they were big enough to be released into the wild.

"That *was* a good weekend," Liz said. "And this one will be too!"

Liz grinned. She had something planned.

This Thanksgiving, Liz was in charge of making one of the Thanksgiving pies. She had already picked out the flavor: cranberry-blueberry pie with a hint of orange and cinnamon. Liz wanted it to be perfect. So she needed to practice. She was going to start this weekend at the cabin. And Amy, Marion, and Ellie could help.

Suddenly, Liz had a thought. Rather than having the girls help, they could each make a pie of their own. This was going to be the best surprise ever!

Are We There Yet?

The Jenkins family van merged onto the highway.

"Who wants to play the alphabet game?" Liz asked her friends.

Marion, Amy, and Ellie were in the way back. Liz and her big brother, Stewart, sat in the two middle row seats. And Liz's parents were up front.

They were on their way to Marigold Lake!

"It's only about an hour drive," Stewart said. "But playing car games makes it feel even shorter."

Ellie sat up straight in her seat. "I'll play!" she said.

"Me too," said Amy.

Marion nodded. "What are the rules?" she asked.

Liz explained. Starting with the letter A, each of them had to find all the letters of the alphabet on objects they passed on the highway. The letters could be on traffic signs, license plates, or billboards.

"Liz and I usually play against each other," Stewart said. "The first person to find all the letters is the winner."

"But we could play as a team!" Liz suggested. "At least for the first game. Ready, set, go!"

Everyone looked out the window. They scanned signs for letters.

"A!" Amy called out. She pointed at a sign that said REST AREA AHEAD.

Marion found the next one on another car's license plate. "B!" she cried, clapping excitedly.

"C!" said Ellie, pointing at a billboard ad for Canoe and Kayak Warehouse.

Mile by mile, they worked their way through the alphabet. The letter J was hard to find. Same with Q.

But X was surprisingly easy. It was on every exit sign.

"There!" Liz called out, pointing to the X on the exit sign for Marigold Lake. "We're almost there!"

At the end of the exit ramp, Liz's dad turned right onto a country road.

Then, just a mile down the road, Liz's dad pulled off into a gravel parking lot. A rustic wooden sign read OTIS ORCHARDS.

Liz turned around in her seat. "We're here!" she said, grinning at her friends.

Ellie looked confused. "What do you mean?" she said. "This isn't the cabin."

Liz opened the van door and unbuckled her seat belt. "You're right," she said. "We just have to make this one stop."

They all got out of the van. Liz led the way over to a farm stand. Beyond it were rows and rows of fruit trees.

"We're going to pick fruit," Liz announced. "For pies!" Liz explained that she needed to practice baking her Thanksgiving pie. "I thought we could each bake one."

Ellie, Marion, and Amy looked at one another. Huge smiles lit up their faces.

Liz's dad came up next to them. "I made pie crusts ahead of time," he told the girls.

"So what kind are we going to make?" Amy asked.

"You each get to choose," Liz replied.

Ellie did a little happy dance. "This is going to be so much fun!"

Marion looked deep in thought already. "There are so many good pie flavors," she said. "What will I pick?"

Liz pointed at a chalkboard sign. It had a list of pick-your-own fruits that were ripe that day. "Well, you could start by *picking* some of those!" Liz said.

Chapter 3

On the Farm

Liz told her friends about her Thanksgiving pie recipe.

"It's a cranberry-blueberry pie," she said. "But it's a little late in the season to pick blueberries. And cranberries don't grow around here. So I brought ingredients from home. I hope you don't think it's unfair that I had a bit of a head start."

Ellie laughed. "Unfair? I'm just so excited to be at an orchard!"

"I can't wait to bake," Marion added. Amy smiled in agreement.

Ellie studied the pick-your-own list. "Hmm. I'm going to choose apple," she said. "I just looooove apple pie."

PICK YOUR OWN Fruits!
• APPLES
• PEARS
• ASIAN PEA
• Pump

Amy pointed to the last item on the sign. "It might sound weird. But my mom makes this great sweet potato pie," she said. "I'm going to call her and get the recipe."

Marion was the last to decide. "Okay," she said finally. "I've made a pumpkin pie before. I think I can remember how to do it."

The girls got directions from the orchard staff about where to pick. Ellie and Amy grabbed baskets to put their apples and sweet potatoes in. Marion grabbed a wagon for her pumpkins.

Then they split up. Liz took Ellie toward the apple trees. Amy and Marion went together in the direction of the pumpkins and sweet potatoes.

In the middle of the apple grove, Ellie stopped at a signpost. "Wow," said Ellie. "There are so many different kinds of apples! How do I choose?"

Liz stepped closer to the sign-post. "Look!" she said. She pointed at smaller writing under each apple type. "This one says 'good for baking.'"

"Golden Delicious!" Ellie said. "Great! I'll get some of those."

Liz and Ellie walked down the path between two rows of apple trees. They stopped near a tree that was loaded with ripe apples. Liz held the basket. Stretching, Ellie could just reach the apples on the lower branches. One by one, she plucked Golden Delicious apples and handed them down to Liz.

Soon they had about a dozen. Liz had to put the heavy basket down.

"That's probably enough," Liz said with a laugh.

Ellie grabbed one side of the handle. Liz took the other. Then they set off to find Marion and Amy.

They found them in the sweet potato section. Marion already had pumpkins in her wagon.

But Amy was looking confused.

"These are sweet potato plants," she said, pointing to the plant label at the end of the row. "But all I see are leafy vines. Where are the sweet potatoes?"

Liz giggled. She knelt down and loosened the soil around one of the plants. Then she grabbed a stem and yanked upward. Out popped a bunch of dirt-covered sweet potatoes!

"Wow!" Amy cried out in surprise. "I did *not* know they grew that way!"

Ellie put an arm around Amy's shoulder. "I didn't know how many kinds of apples there are," she said.

Marion pointed at her pumpkins. "Well, *I* do not know how many pumpkins I'll need for pumpkin pie. I sure hope this will be enough."

Marion heaved a large pumpkin
up out of the wagon. It was even
bigger than her head.

Liz, Amy, and Ellie laughed.

"That should do it," Liz said.

Chapter 4

Pie Problems

"Squee-onk! Squee-onk!"

It was bright and early Saturday morning at the cabin. The day's "alarm clock" was going off. Outside on the lake, flocks of geese honked as they took flight.

Liz rolled over in her bed. She peeked over the side at her friends in sleeping bags on the floor of her room. Ellie was rubbing her eyes.

"I forgot that sound," Ellie said sleepily.

Liz laughed. She heard giggles from inside Amy's and Marion's sleeping bags too. Everyone was awake now!

Liz looked out the window. In the morning sunshine, the trees around the lake were bright with color. Lots of yellow, but also rusty oranges and fiery reds. It was even more colorful here than back in Santa Vista.

"Let's go on a walk after breakfast," Liz said. "The fall colors are amazing here!"

Her friends agreed that was a great idea.

The girls got up and got dressed.

They gathered around the table in the cabin's kitchen. Liz's dad put out oatmeal and toppings: nuts, cinnamon, granola, and frozen berries. Amy, Marion, and Ellie excitedly served themselves.

Meanwhile, Liz stared at the berries. They reminded her of her pie recipe. She was really eager to start practicing.

Oh, but . . . Liz had already suggested going for a walk. All through breakfast, she felt torn.

"You know what?" Liz said when they were done eating. "You three go on without me. I'm going to stay in and make a practice pie."

Amy, Marion, and Ellie looked disappointed. "Are you sure?" Ellie asked.

"We can wait and go later," Amy suggested.

Liz shook her head. "No, that's okay," she said. "You go. It's beautiful outside." Liz didn't want to keep her friends from enjoying the lake. "I just can't wait to see how this recipe turns out."

Marion quickly switched into planning mode. "All right, how about this?" she began. "We'll go for a walk. Then, when we get back, we'll make a picnic for lunch. All four of us."

The girls agreed that was a good plan.

So Marion, Ellie, and Amy headed out toward the path along the lake. And Liz got out her mixing bowl and ingredients.

She looked at the recipe for her cranberry-blueberry pie.

CRANBERRY-BLUEBERRY PIE

INGREDIENTS

• Blueberries
• Cranberries
• Sugar
• Cornstarch
• Cinnamon sticks
• Orange juice

CRUST

DIRECTIONS

Combine all ingredients in a saucepan. Cook over medium heat until mixture begins to boil. Stir occasionally, 12 to 14 minutes

"Sounds easy enough," Liz said to herself.

She put frozen cranberries and frozen blueberries into a saucepan. She added sugar, cinnamon, orange juice, and a bit of cornstarch.

Liz stirred it and turned up the heat. Now it just needed to boil.

"Dad?" Liz called. "Where are the pie crusts?"

Mr. Jenkins dug into a shopping bag they'd brought from home. "They're in here somewhere," he said.

He searched one bag. Then another. Then another. But no pie crusts.

Finally, Liz's mom called out from the pantry. "Here they are! I unpacked them last night."

Liz breathed a sigh of relief. "Thanks, Mom!" she said, taking one of the crusts.

Then Liz hurried back to the stove. She had to stir the berry mixture.

But before Liz saw it, she smelled it.

The scent of burning berries!

Headed South

Liz's pie mixture was so burnt it was stuck to the bottom of the saucepan.

Liz moaned. "I left it for too long without stirring!" she said.

Luckily, they had extra berries. So Liz let the mixture cool. She cleaned out the saucepan. And she started all over.

Her second try went better. She stirred the berry mixture as it came to a low boil. Then she poured the filling into the pie crust.

That's when she spotted the measuring cup full of sugar on the table.

Wait. Had she forgotten to put the sugar in?

Liz took a taste. *Bleh!* The tartness of the cranberries was overpowering. She had definitely skipped the sugar!

Liz slumped into a chair. How had she messed up *again*?

"It's okay," her dad told her. "I made extra crusts. You can try again."

But Liz was feeling too frustrated now. She needed a break. "I'll try later," she said glumly.

Just then, her friends breezed in through the screen door.

"You three are just in time," Liz said.

"For pie?" Ellie asked hopefully.

Liz shook her head. "No," she said. "To take my mind off pie." Liz told them about her mess-ups. "Let's pack our picnic!"

Liz's mom helped them make sandwiches. Amy loaded the picnic basket. Ellie grabbed the picnic blanket.

Soon Liz was leading the way to her favorite picnic spot. It was halfway around the lake on a sandy area by the water.

From their blanket, they had a clear view of the whole lake. Sun glinted off the ripples on the water. Liz took a deep breath of the fresh pine-scented air. She was feeling better already.

Liz took a bite of her hummus and tomato sandwich.

"Squee-onk! Squee-onk!"

Far off down the lake, a huge flock of geese took off from the water, all at once!

"Hey!" said Ellie. "You think they're the ones who woke us up this morning?"

Liz laughed. "Probably," she said.

"There must be a hundred of them," Marion noted.

They watched as the geese flew their way. Honking loudly, they whooshed overhead and kept on going.

"I think that way is south," Amy said. "Maybe they're leaving for the winter."

Ellie waved after them. "Bye, geese! Have a nice flight!"

The girls finished eating. They lounged on their blanket. Then Liz showed them how to skip stones on the water.

Finally, they headed back to the cabin.

When they got to the Jenkins' dock, Amy stopped in her tracks. "Look!" she cried. She pointed at a lone goose in the lake.

"He must be part of that flock we saw," Ellie said.

The goose stretched out his wings as if to take flight. He flapped and honked. *"Squee-onk!"*

But he wasn't lifting off. Instead, his wings were splashing water around.

The girls watched as the goose tried again. He flapped a little longer and honked a little louder. But he didn't get any air.

Liz turned to look at her friends. "Is he okay?" she asked.

Goose Food

"What if he got left behind?" Amy asked.

"That flock is far away by now," Marion pointed out. "If he doesn't catch up . . ." Her voice trailed off.

"He'll miss flying south for the winter!" Ellie cried. "Oh no!"

Liz thought the goose looked a little weak. "Maybe he just needs some food," she suggested. "Maybe we should try to feed him."

But what did geese eat, anyway?

Liz and the girls hurried inside the cabin. Liz explained to her mom what they'd seen.

"Here," Mrs. Jenkins said. "Use my laptop. You can do a search for geese and their favorite foods."

The girls typed in their search. They got lots of results.

"How about bread crumbs?" Ellie asked. "Isn't that what people feed to ducks?"

Amy pointed to some text on the screen. "Actually this says that bread isn't good for ducks or geese," she replied. "It's too high in sugar. But here's a list of good choices."

- Stems
- Roots
- Seeds
- Grains
- Berries
- Insects
- Aquatic Plants

GEESE

While Amy, Marion, and Ellie read, Liz's nose picked up the scent of her failed pies. There was still a slightly burnt smell in the cabin. And nearby on the table was Liz's second failure, the sugarless pie.

The sight of it made Liz frustrated again.

She picked up the pie. She carried it out onto the porch of the cabin where she set it down on a chair.

"There," Liz said. "Out of sight, out of mind."

Back inside, Marion had an idea about goose food. "The oatmeal from breakfast!" Marion said. "That's a grain. Let's see if he likes that."

Liz hurried to the pantry. She grabbed the box of rolled oats and then ran back out into the kitchen.

Ellie, Marion, and Amy were all huddled at the window, peering out.

"He's gone!" Ellie was saying. "The goose is gone."

Liz ran over to see. Ellie was right. Out on the water, there was no sign of the goose.

"Did he fly away?" Liz asked. "Maybe he's fine after all."

Marion stepped out onto the porch to get a better view.

"Wait!" Marion called. "There he is! Liz! He's in your yard. And he's coming this way!"

Chapter 7

The Uninvited Guest

Liz opened the box of oats.

"Here!" she said to her friends. "Everybody take some." Liz poured some oats into their hands.

Then the four of them went out onto the porch. The goose was down on the lawn, snacking on grass.

Slowly, quietly, Liz led the way down the steps. They didn't want to scare the goose away.

The goose looked up at them.

"*Squee-onk!*" he honked loudly. The girls jumped and stopped in their tracks.

"Okay," said Liz. "I guess that's close enough!"

The girls tossed some oats in the goose's direction. They rained down onto the grass a few feet in front of him. The goose waddled over and poked at them with his bill. Then the goose straightened up. He waddled on, past the oats. And then past the girls.

"Where is he going?" Liz whispered out of the corner of her mouth.

The goose came to the bottom of the cabin steps. He flapped his wings as he hopped up the first, second, and third steps. He was going up onto the porch!

The girls followed at a distance. They watched as the goose got to the top of the stairs and then waddled right up to a chair.

The chair on which Liz had set her pie.

"Squee-onk! Squee-onk! Squee-onk!" the goose honked loudly.

"Liz," Marion whispered, "he wants your pie."

Ellie pulled at Liz's shirt sleeve. "Berries!" she cried. "Berries were on that list of foods that geese eat!"

"Really?" Liz replied. She had been distracted when the girls were reading the info. "He wants my yucky sugarless pie?"

Amy gasped. "That's perfect!" she said. "Remember how we read that bread is bad for geese? It said it's too high in sugar."

Liz laughed. "Yeah, well that pie is definitely *not* high in sugar."

Suddenly, the goose plunged his bill straight into the center of the pie. He took a huge bite of the pie filling. He gobbled it down, then took another. And another.

"He likes it!" Liz cried in awe. It was hard to believe. But that goose was clearly enjoying her pie.

The girls watched as the goose ate up all the pie filling. He wasn't the neatest eater. Globs of pie landed on the chair and on the porch and all around.

Soon all that remained in the tin were hunks of pie crust.

Then the goose turned and hopped back down the steps. He waddled calmly back toward the lake.

Watching him go, the girls couldn't help laughing. "What just happened?" Ellie asked.

"I don't know," Liz replied. "But I think I know what we should call him."

"What?" asked Marion.

Liz looked back at the messy tin. "Pie."

Chapter 8

Pie's Second Chance

The next morning, the girls ate their bagels on the porch. From there, they could see Pie out on the lake. He was happily swimming about ten feet beyond the end of the dock.

"Is it just me, or does he look stronger today?" Amy asked.

Liz looked closer. Maybe he did. "We haven't seen him try to fly though," Liz pointed out.

Marion nudged Liz. "It's a good thing you baked that pie," she said. "We might not have tried giving him berries."

Liz nodded. It *was* lucky that her imperfect pie had turned out to be Pie's perfect meal. Suddenly Liz had an idea. Maybe she should make him another one?

Right now, Pie looked fine. But surely he'd need to eat again. And he'd need a lot of energy for his trip south.

That reminded her. "Do you think his flock will come back for him?" Liz asked.

All four girls looked up at the sky over the lake. There was no sign of the other geese.

After breakfast, the girls brought their breakfast plates inside. They decided to get started baking their pies. That way, they could serve them for dessert after Sunday dinner.

They gathered all
the pie ingredients.
Marion scooped
the seeds out of
her pumpkins.
Amy started
peeling sweet potatoes.
Ellie washed her apples.
And Liz decided
she *was* going to make
another pie for Pie. No
sugar. Only this time,
on purpose.

Liz was pulling out the pie crusts when she heard it.

Through an open pantry window came the faraway but unmistakable sound . . . of geese. Lots and lots of geese.

"Do you hear that?" Liz called to her friends.

Amy, Marion, and Ellie stood still and listened. The honking grew louder.

"They're coming back!" Ellie exclaimed.

Together, the girls ran out onto the porch and down the steps.

At the far end of the lake, over the tall trees, the lead geese came into view.

They were followed by many more. The flock swooped down low over the lake. In a flash, they were flying past the Jenkins' dock.

Out on the lake, Pie was flapping his wings!

"Pie!" Liz called out. "Now's your chance!"

"He's trying!" Marion said.

They watched him, holding their breath. Slowly, slowly, Pie lifted up off the surface of the water. At first, he seemed to struggle. But with each flap of his wings, Pie looked stronger and smoother. He was doing it!

"Go, Pie, go!" Ellie cried.

Higher and higher, Pie rose up into the sky. He flapped feverishly until, at last, he fell into formation at the back of the flock.

The girls erupted into cheers.

"It's official!" Liz announced. "Pie is in the sky!"

Chapter 9

Goose-berry Pie

That evening, Liz's mom and dad made veggie burgers and tofu dogs on the grill. They ate around the firepit. After dinner, they would all pitch in to clean and pack up. Then they would load everything into the van and head back to Santa Vista.

But first, they capped off their weekend with a very special dessert buffet.

Up on the porch, four beautiful pies were set out on the table. Each of the bakers was very proud of her creation. They had even named the flavors and made labels.

Amy's pie was labeled MOM'S SWEET POTATO PIE. It was her mom's recipe, after all!

Ellie's pie was labeled ASTONISHING APPLE.

Marion's was PERFECTLY PUMPKIN.

And Liz had decided to name hers GOOSE-BERRY PIE. Marion pointed out that a gooseberry was a real fruit that kind of looked and tasted like a grape. But Liz thought gooseberry was funny. As in, the type of berries a goose likes to eat.

Everyone took tiny slices of each flavor pie. That way, they could taste all of them.

Liz tasted her friends' pies first. She loved them all.

Ellie's apple pie was cinnamon-y, with a hint of lemon zest.

Marion's pumpkin pie was smooth and airy, with the perfect amount of pumpkin spice.

Amy's sweet potato pie was a yummy combination of brown sugar and ginger.

Liz took a bite of her own pie last.

She wasn't sure Pie would have liked *this* Goose-berry Pie. She had added the sugar this time. And the crust was baked to a golden brown. It tasted very different from Pie's pie.

But Liz liked it. The orange from the orange juice. The tartness of the cranberries. The sweetness from the blueberries. They went together well, she thought.

Liz looked around. Did anyone else like it?

"Yum!" said Stewart, taking a bite. "Liz, this is *good*!"

Liz beamed. That was a big compliment coming from her brother.

Ellie, Amy, and Marion nodded in agreement. Everyone seemed to like the Goose-berry Pie.

Even so, Liz thought she'd practice making it a couple more times before Thanksgiving.

Just in case!